The Letter of the Apostle Paul

to

The Church at LAODICEA

as Transmitted to
Hon. Steven R. Frances

by

ROBERT F SIMMS

This is a work of fiction. Names, places and incidents are either the product of the author's imagination or are actual persons, places and incidents used fictitiously, and any resemblance to actual persons, living or dead, or their actions, or to churches, universities, events, or locales is entirely coincidental.

ISBN: 978-0-9995929-6-0
Published in the United States by
Robert F. Simms
Greer, South Carolina

Contents

1 • Rome, Early A.D. 61

He looked over the freshly scribed letter one more time to make certain there were no errors. All appeared to be well. The ink was of better quality than some he had resigned himself to using here, and the parchment was a welcome substitute for cheaper papyrus. He evened up the several sheets of the letter and looked again at the opening Greek words:

> **Paul an apostle of Jesus Christ by the will of God to the saints which are at Laodicea…**

He reached for one of the new goatskin covers a friend had made for him, a beautifully made piece of leatherwork and a fitting container for the well crafted letter it would contain. He opened it on the side and slid the pages of the letter inside it. There was no need to seal it, and he didn't have a seal at this point anyway. He simply handed the goatskin to the man attending him and nodded. Delivery had been prearranged. In a week or two, perhaps three, it would reach its destination.

2 • USA, MARCH, 2019

THE NAME ON MY DESK nameplate says Steven R. Frances, Judge, but it's no longer on the desk in my chambers. When I retired I put the name plate on my desk at home, a reminder of the thirty-five years I spent hearing low level criminal cases and civil matters not exceeding $20,000.00 in claims. After completing law school way back in the previous century, I spent my first five years of professional life trying to make it as a small-town lawyer, finally realizing that there were both too many other lawyers in the area and also too few clients for the kind of law I preferred to practice. After a few timely contacts and a lot of divine grace, I got the opportunity to move to the other side of the bar and listen to lawyers' arguments rather than make them.

My history in the law and the courts has little bearing on the story I'm going to tell you, except to explain the devotion I have to the importance of evidence and the concept of making informed judgments on the basis of that evidence. That standard will be critical to your evaluation of my tale.

And, I mention my vocation in the law as a preface to telling you about my avocation, which is biblical theology. As a Baptist layman with a family background thoroughly saturated with theological practitioners—ministers and professors—I have always considered myself called to my vocation to pay the bills and called to my avocation to fulfil a need of my spirit. I didn't go to a theological school, but I did a lot of reading in the field. A *lot*. My younger brother, Patrick, a pastor in a nearby city, has a seminary doctorate. I was two years into my law practice when he began his theological education, and I asked him if I might borrow and read his textbooks during the semester after he completed those courses. I fit this reading into my schedule without a great deal of difficulty because when I left the law office every day I didn't carry the job home with me. I had plenty of time in the evenings when I could have been reading novels, but I chose to teach myself church history, theology, and even biblical languages.

Out of this self-study I've been able to contribute writings to Baptist publications from time to time, and to teach the Bible in my own church and occasionally in regional conferences. And, my somewhat dual profession throughout my years as first lawyer and then judge helps explain why, when I left the job I did for money, I started pursuing in earnest what I had always done for love. Over the years I had come up with books I wanted to write. Retirement was an open door of new opportunity to fulfil my longstanding "second calling."

One of those books was a study in theophanies—those Old Testament manifestations of God before the event of the incarnation—and how they help prove the reality of the trinity as a biblical doctrine. Now there's a best seller for certain. I was also hoping to market the three volumes I had written during my judicial career about the drama of small claims civil court cases, surely another page turner. Fortunately, my retirement income was sufficient for my needs.

What I'm going to describe to you, at least my role in it, began in 2020, the year that would go down in world history books as the year of the Coronavirus. People all over the world went insane as governments stoked the fires of fear and ruined the economies of whole countries in an attempt to stop the unstoppable, a virus that spread much like the common cold—which no one has ever been able to prevent. Admittedly a small percentage of people who contracted Covid-19, the new name for what you got when you were exposed to the Coronavirus (technically, SARS-CoV-2), died from the disease. But it appeared that all over the world all but a few leaders made the mistake of not sufficiently weighing the cost of saving a few lives against the cost of demolishing their economies, which itself was going to cost lives, and did.

What happened to me in the early summer of the year of the Coronavirus, 2020, had nothing to do with the pandemic *per se*, but I mention it for two reasons.

One reason is that what happened to me was just as powerful an experience as coming very close to dying earlier that year. In March, I came down with Covid-19 and spent a week in the hospital praying every eight seconds for just one more breath. I exaggerate a bit, because I never had to be put in the ICU, which by some measures was a death sentence: almost no one who got that far recovered. By June, in fact, I was mostly well and hoping just to cruise through the year with no more crises, in fact no more excitement at all, just rest and writing. Instead, I was drawn into a secret that spanned a long, long time and that confronted me with a more significant decision than I had ever made in my career as a judge.

The other reason I mention the year of the Coronavirus is the dramatic illustration it offered of the absolute need of both "experts" and the public to have evidence to back up their actions. You'll see why that was so important in a moment.

After surviving Covid-19, I was counting on a placid summer getting back to 100%. I was spending my time divided between the physically passive pursuit of writing books and the more active pursuit of motorcycle riding. My wife and I called my riding "wind therapy." It was also vibration therapy, a curative for recurring back problems, probably from sitting too much and reading theology books. As I said, I had in mind several books I wanted to write, now that I had all the time in the world on my hands.

The previous year, I had conceived of an article for our denominational magazine on the subject of the 1st century church at Laodicea and the letter Paul wrote to that church, a letter that did not survive Paul's own time. I had lit on the idea of writing an essay-length piece on the subject after my early morning Bible study one day in my own little "upper room" at home. It was, and is, my habit to rise at 6:00 a.m. or so, pour a cup of coffee, mount the stairs to the bonus room of our house that is stuffed with my library—my two libraries, home and now erstwhile office—my computers and a comfortable chair, and sit with my Bible for an hour or more.

That morning, in late January of 2019, I was reading in Colossians, and I became unusually interested in wondering about Paul's mention of having written to the church at Laodicea. This letter, unlike John's short paragraph in Revelation that also mentions the church, disappeared from history. I wanted to bone up on the subject.

As often I did, I called my brother, Patrick, and ran the idea by him. He was off work that day and was puttering around his house. It was raining and he had reluctantly cancelled his fishing trip, and he was looking for something to do. So he offered to come over late morning, have lunch and then bat around the Laodicean idea with me at my house. Fortunately for both of us he was a mere thirty miles away, and he arrived in time for us to get an early seat at my favorite Mexican restaurant. After splitting fajitas we retreated to my home.

"Is this going to be a book, or what?" he began.

"Dunno," I said. "You know me. I've got two books already started and I sort of stalled on them when I got interested in this idea."

"When you told me you were looking into the Laodicean thing I had a few minutes to Google it," Patrick said. "I admit I didn't know much about it. Nobody ever mentioned it at the seminary, and I never really ran across it in any texts. It's probably there, somewhere in my library, and I'm sure a footnote or two in a commentary on Colossians must have mentioned it."

"Maybe, maybe not," I said. "I have some of your texts from church history, and I went back and looked in them. No references to the Laodicean letter."

"Really?" he said.

"Really. I had to Google it, too."

"What would we do without Google?" he said.

"Probably we'd be a lot less tracked on the Internet."

"True. I've started using one of those alternative search engines that doesn't keep records."

"Me, too. When I say, 'Google,' I usually mean DuckDuckGo.com. Try it." He wrote down the site name.

"Anyway," I said, "I started out with the basic idea that people don't know what happened to the letter. But that isn't quite all there is to it, apparently."

"There have been two or three letters, haven't there?" he said.

"Two, as far as I can tell," I said. "Both of them long ago debunked and dismissed."

"Can we brew some coffee while we talk?" Patrick said.

"Sure," I said. "It's time for my after-lunch cup anyway." I got up and went into the kitchen to my Keurig coffee maker and selected some strong blends for a couple of cups. When they were finished brewing in about a minute, we sat back down with them.

"From what I found on the Internet after you called, there's a lot of info on Laodicea from other historical sources," said Patrick. "You've got the Roman records, the church fathers, blah, blah, blah. Most of it gets referenced by preachers when they do sermons on Revelation. But I've never heard a sermon—one that I recall, anyway—on that reference to Laodicea in Colossians, though."

"Me, either," I said, "but then neither of us is exposed to a lot of sermons outside our own churches."

"So, if you start with the Bible as the most reliable document on the subject of the letter, basically you have just Colossians and Revelation," he said.

"That's it," I said. "You've got the first mention of the letter itself in Colossians 4, where Paul says the Christians at Colossae should read the epistle from Laodicea. And nobody knows of any correspondence from the Colossian church back to Paul saying that their neighbors in Laodicea hadn't heard from him."

"But we wouldn't, would we," he argued. It was a statement rather than a question. "I mean, for instance, Paul told the Corinthian church he had heard from them after he wrote 1 Corinthians, but we don't have that letter. I mean, nobody preserved it: it didn't have the force of scripture. Paul wouldn't have had their letter copied for any kind of distribution. It was apparently just a personal letter telling him about issues they had, or their reaction to what he had written them before. In 1 Corinthians."

"True," I said, "so I don't suppose we can rest any argument on our lack of a letter or message from Colossae."

"So where does that leave you?" he said.

"I suppose it leaves me with the assumption that's been made since sometime in the first millennium, that if there *were* a letter by Paul to the Laodiceans, it simply didn't survive the first century."

"What do you mean, if there *were* one?" he said.

"Well, some people don't think he actually wrote it, that he was planning to write it when he mentioned it to the Colossians, but then didn't. Reasons unknown."

"But then, would his saying that he wrote to Laodicea have rendered the letter to the Colossians unauthoritative?" he asked.

"Hmm. You mean, when the church nailed down the canon of the New Testament?"

"Or before, in fact."

"So if they knew that there never had been a Laodicean letter, would they have omitted Colossians from the canon because it referred to a non-existent writing?"

"Yeah. It would have been an error," he said.

"I see that, and I'm not saying I give any credence to the thought that the Laodicean letter never existed in the first place. It's just one idea."

"Well, after you brought up the whole idea on the phone, I did some reading about the Council of Florence," said Patrick.

"When was that? Remind me."

"Fifteenth century. They finalized the canon. And from what I gathered, the prevailing idea there was that the Laodicean letter simply hadn't been meant by God to be in the New Testament," he said. "They didn't have a letter they thought was genuine."

We mulled over that a minute. "Okay," I said, "what do

we know about the Church at Laodicea?"

"You go first," he said. "I'm not up to speed yet."

I flipped through a few printouts of web pages I had researched.

"Well, to begin with, Paul's letter to the Church at Colossae was probably written in A.D. 62 from Rome. He was kind of on house arrest. And he had people with him, sort of coming and going. Luke, Epaphras, Tychicus and others."

"I think the date could be a year or two either way," said Patrick. "Scholars differ."

"I know, but I like 62. It fits with related facts better."

"Okay, go with A.D. 62, then."

"So, working from what he said to the Colossians, it looks like Laodicea had a heresy developing. A Christological heresy. In Colossians 2, Paul says he was concerned about them, particularly because they needed to understand the person and work of Christ better."

Patrick took his Bible and found the passage. "Okay, he says he has 'conflict' about Laodicea, and then he says they need to acknowledge the 'mystery of God and of the Father and of Christ,' so nobody would 'beguile' them with 'enticing words.' Okay, I'll agree with you. Looks like they had at least an incomplete understanding of Jesus."

"Because?" I said.

"Because—Paul hadn't been there himself. He hadn't

taught them," said Patrick.

"Right. Like he said, they hadn't 'seen his face.'"

"So he wrote them a letter."

"To teach them some things they didn't know. Their ignorance had probably led to some conduct that was going to get them in trouble."

"But," Patrick countered, "there's precious little in Colossians 2 about this. If it was, in fact, a Christological heresy, wouldn't there have been more? Wouldn't Paul have explained what he meant?"

"In Colossians?" I said. "I don't think so. He would have written that to the Laodiceans, themselves."

"Okay, I'll agree with that," said Patrick. "And the rest of what we can conclude about the heretical idea we get from Revelation."

"A lot of it, yes," I said. "If you take the date of John's writing Revelation as between A.D. 90 and 95, it was about thirty years from Colossians to Revelation, where John wrote down what Christ told him to say to Laodicea. And of course, he famously said the Laodicean church was 'neither cold nor hot.'"

"And you're thinking that their being lukewarm is a direct result of whatever was going on as early as A.D. 62," said Patrick.

"Right. These things often take a generation to develop."

"Makes sense," he said. "I did a sermon series in the

letters to the seven churches of Revelation last year."

"I remember," I said. "I meant to come over and hear some of it, but I couldn't get out of obligations at my church."

"You're forgiven," he said. "It was probably an eminently forgettable series, anyway."

"I doubt that," I said. "You're probably going to put it into a book." We regularly made self-abnegating remarks, baiting each other for compliments. It was a habit that went way back into our early professional years.

"Did you offer an opinion in that series about the big problem at Laodicea?" I asked.

"Sure. I didn't bring any study notes with me, but basically I said that they had achieved local social acceptance. They were economically successful—that whole thing about the commodity of black wool and their banking—and they had assumed that God had blessed them because of their community status. Like the Jews did, before Christ."

"How do you interpret Jesus' word 'lukewarm,'" I said.

"Oh, I've always agreed with interpreters who take that to mean they had stopped making disciples. They weren't *fiery* evangelists."

"My view, too," I said. "So what I'm thinking is that we can read back into the Colossian letter that the churches in Laodicea were drifting into evangelistic apathy because of this heresy: not understanding Christ properly."

"But in what way?" said Patrick. "I mean, what deficiency in their beliefs about Christ would account for being lukewarm about evangelism?"

"Well, it's got to be some idea about Christ that didn't acknowledge their obligation to fulfill the great commission."

"I don't know," he said. "I would agree, except that I don't know that we know they had enough of the gospel writings by that time to even have the 'great commission' in front of them."

"Maybe they did," I said. "Some scholars think Mark was written as early as A.D. 55, which would have provided several years for copies to have circulated."

"Well, that may be a little early. Most sources I've studied date it more like A.D. 67."

"Maybe, but in that case, Mark would have used some sources that were being put together much earlier."

Patrick took up the debate. "But," he said, "*but:* remember that the gospel of Mark originally ended right after the account of the resurrection. He didn't have a 'great commission' account."

I broke in. "Which may mean only that Mark *did* write an ending but that his own ending was lost before the first copies were made. Because everybody agrees that somebody else wrote the last few verses later—the verses we have today."

"Okay," he said, "true, but we're getting off track. We don't know that the Laodiceans had a written gospel."

"Or that they didn't," I said. "But whoever first preached the gospel in Laodicea *had* to have said something about witnessing and making disciples."

"But we don't know that, either," said Patrick. "Which brings us back to Paul's saying he really wanted Laodicea to have some personal teaching from him."

We sipped and finished our coffee and ruminated on that thought for a minute.

"Okay," I said. "So, we're agreed that they didn't know enough about what Paul and the other apostles were teaching about Jesus. I'm still not certain they didn't have a gospel, and I'm reasonably certain some of Paul's earlier letters had been copied and circulated in the region by A.D. 62. Is there anything else that would account for Laodicea's cooling off?"

"Well, you've always got the obvious factor of persecution," said Patrick. "It was, after all, the Roman Empire, and Nero was the Emperor."

"Okay, so you have growing persecution for not saying, 'Nero is Lord.'"

"Right," he said. He was cogitating, and I could see a shift in thought coming. "Okay, all of this probably suggests what Paul *wrote* to the Laodiceans. But still, what happened to the letter? None of this explains that."

"I'm still getting there," I said. "But I have a theory."

"Which, if we're going to keep this conversation going, I'm probably going to have to continue to another day. I promised my wife I'd take her out for supper, and I'm going to have to get back."

"Okay, but here's where I'm going with it. It starts with the person most likely to have been the intended recipient of the letter."

"I would presume the pastor," he said.

"Me, too. Which would probably have been Nymphas. He's mentioned in Colossians 4:15. The church was in his house."

"Probably, yes."

"What if he didn't get it? The letter?"

Patrick's eyebrows went up. We both thought about the concept for a beat.

"Or got it and didn't like it?" said Patrick.

"Maybe," I said. "Like I said, I'm still working on that."

"Well, keep working," he said. Patrick went into the kitchen and rinsed out his coffee cup.

"When is the article going to come out?" he called out.

"I haven't even written it yet!" I said. "I'm going to pitch it to the magazine editor and see what he says. I may have to write it in two parts."

"Well, you want to get together again and hash out the rest of your ideas?" said Patrick. "I'll be ready for tamales by next Friday."

"Definitely," I said.

"Why don't you come my way, then?" he said. "There's a new restaurant opened up I want to try. Tamal Café."

"Sounds good," I said, and we agreed on a time.

After Patrick left, I sat down and churned out a draft of what would become the first half of the article, from what I had already researched and from the reasoning and the nuances of the conversation we had just had.

I expanded on the subject of persecution under Nero, and Part One ended this way:

> Aggressive evangelism attracts the negative attention of religiously intolerant governments, but passive congregations give little offense to a contrary world and often make it possible for them to survive physically.
>
> The church that neither flaunts its rejection of the claims of despotic government nor boldly announces its allegiance to an alternative King may fly under the radar for a prolonged time. Probably the Laodiceans' realization that they should go along to get along prompted the kind of thinking that resulted in a softened, moderated view of the deity of Jesus Christ and his claim of absolute lordship over their lives. Why invite ostracism or persecution?
>
> When Paul wrote to Laodicea, their moderate theology was a matter of concern. By the time of John's exile on

Patmos and his visions of the exalted Christ, the situation in Laodicea had reached critical mass.

— *In part 2: what did the Letter to Laodicea say, and what happened to it?*

3 • ITALY, 1ST CENTURY

A MESSENGER in a nondescript tunic with leggings and shoes for warmth made his way down through the bustling streets, through the area of the Palatium and over to the Via Asinaria, finally reaching the outskirts of the great city and going toward the province of Samnium and beyond.

The road was good—one of the benefits of being swept into Roman rule—and the frequency of contingents of soldiers rendered it safe to travel. His first destination was nearly 5,000 stadia away, not that anybody much measured things that way. It was about 530 Roman miles. In simpler terms, it would take him about two weeks to get there, or as much as three, presuming that he could find a seat in a redda at the edge of Rome. Carriage businesses were usually just outside city walls.

Fortunately, the messenger found transportation just past the city's growing demarcation. He then made his way southeast toward the coast and the province of Calabria. The road went south to the west of the mountains more than half the way, then east through a pass at Vennsia, and through little towns as it approached the Adriatic.

More than once, the driver fed and watered his horses at a river and passengers slept in the open or in the carriage itself with whatever blankets they had before going on early the next morning. When they were able to find inns, for nights a bit more restful, they stocked up on dried foods and forged on. Finally the outskirts of Brundisium came into view as they crested the Italian peninsula's southern stretches, and passengers began to feel the relief of the end of their bumpy, overland trek.

The sparkling sun off the rippled waters revealed a busy port with numerous vessels, and the man in the nondescript tunic bearing an expensive goatskin folder tucked in the pack on his back climbed out of the carriage at the city's edge and walked through the residential streets, then the markets, and then shipping businesses until he came to the docks.

He had been this way before, and he walked south until he came to a landing where one of several merchant ships that came and went from Asia was docked. He had been to Ephesus twice this way and to Cyprus once, via such ships, which often sold affordable passage to a few travelers. Within an hour, he had located a vessel that had a space available.

The crewman booking the passengers quoted him the price and took his coins.

"Name?" said the crewman.

"Drusus," said the messenger.

The crewman scrawled the name in the ship's log and waved Drusus onboard. He located his sleeping stall below deck, but kept his pack with him as he came back to the main deck and found a place to sit while the last of the cargo was being hoisted aboard. The ship carried what looked to him like forty souls, most of them crew. There were eight passengers, including him. By mid afternoon they were underway.

Days of tossing lay ahead, if weather was typical, and Drusus prayed silently for calm seas and clear skies. They would hug the coastline often until they skirted the coast of Achaia, then lose sight of land for a day until they began dodging islands as they headed toward Miletus. If all went well, he might set foot on dry land within the week.

The last night aboard ship the captain told the passengers that Miletus was only a few hours distant and they should make port by morning. Most of them bedded down for a few hours of sleep around midnight. Drusus stayed on the port side enjoying the moonlight and then turned in himself.

He awoke sometime around the change of watch before dawn and immediately became aware something was amiss. His pack, which he had sometimes used as a very uncomfortable pillow, was behind him as he awoke on his side. Vaguely Drusus recalled having moved it there in the middle of the night, and he had used a spare cloak, rolled up tightly, for his pillow instead. But the pack was open, and he was sure he had closed it.

He rifled through the few possessions in the leather container and quickly realized the goatskin folder was gone.

In a few minutes, it would be light, the passengers would be stirring, and he would have more difficulty in confronting someone about his missing possession. He had to move quickly, and right now. He prayed for wisdom and insight.

No one else appeared to be awake as the messenger got up silently and went slowly along at the feet of the other passengers, seven in all, who were in stalls around his. It was possible, of course, that one of the crew had come into the passenger area and looked for things to steal. If the messenger didn't find the packet among the passengers, he would take the matter to the captain, but he hoped that wouldn't be necessary. A captain would discipline a crewman, of course, but not without knowing fairly certainly the crewman had committed theft. And he would be initially very doubtful of a passenger's complaint about lost items. He would defend his crew unless solid evidence of theft could be shown. The messenger had nothing, nothing except a lost goatskin packet. He had no proof he had even come aboard with it, much less anything to show that anyone on board had taken it.

Of the seven other passengers, two were women, sleeping with their husbands. Drusus thought it unlikely that any of these four was the culprit. One of the couples had a teenage child; Drusus eliminated him, too. That left three men. He could just make out the features of the man in the stall nearest his. The man appeared to be about fifty. Drusus recalled seeing him amidship a few days before, limping slightly, probably from an old injury. Something told Drusus to eliminate him from suspicion. The something was probably Someone, and Drusus thanked God for speaking silently to his heart.

That left two men. One of them Drusus had met the first day onboard, barely an adult, a young man exploring the world, perhaps with his father's money. He appeared to have very good shoes and several quality bags with clothes and other things. Nothing about him suggested he needed what anyone else had.

The remaining man, no more than thirty, was leaning against rolled up blankets in the stall's corner, snoring slightly. Drusus made no noise, but the man woke with a start, and pulled himself tightly into the corner as he saw the messenger's figure in the gloom below deck on a moonlit predawn.

"What do you want?" he cried out in a whisper.

"You know what I want," said Drusus.

"No, I don't," said the man defensively.

But Drusus had lived long enough, known enough people, good and bad, and studied them as a matter of habit, that he knew when someone was lying. In addition to that, the Spirit inside him who had narrowed the field to this one man among all the passengers and crew, said clearly to his alert mind, "This is the one."

"Yes, you do," said Drusus, "and you have more to worry about than me. The God who made heaven and earth also made the sea on which this ship sails, and in spite of the courage and skill of the captain who commands her, the one who commands the sea can toss every man and woman aboard *over*board. Or just one of them. Will it be you?"

The man blanched, such that even in the barest of light his skin proclaimed itself bloodless. Even so, once more he tried denying he knew what Drusus' approach was about.

"I don't know what you want. Do you want to rob me?" said the man.

"Out of your own mouth you speak your own crime," said Drusus. "Give me the goatskin folder, and pray that God will forgive you for laying your hands on it."

At that, the man fainted. The messenger could see that he had, for his head dropped to the side and he slumped toward the floor.

Quickly, Drusus stepped to the unconscious figure and felt in the dark for any packs he might have near him. There was only one, which the man had been using to help him stay propped up. The messenger pulled it toward himself and felt, more than looked, into the pack in the dark. Instantly, he found the goatskin.

He pulled it out and opened it, feeling for the sheets inside. They were all there. He tucked the goatskin under his left arm and reached out with his right, slapping the man on his face, just enough to wake him.

The man woke and jerked back into the corner as he realized Drusus was right in front of him. His eyes went down to the lightly colored goatskin and came back up to the messenger's gaze.

In a trembling voice the man said, "I only took it because it's new and it would probably bring me enough coin in port to eat for a day or two."

Drusus looked at the man's clothes, saw the ratty condition of the pack he had, noticed he had no boots or shoes, only worn sandals in the chill of the season, and at sea, no less. And he was very thin. He judged that the man was telling the truth. He had probably spent his last silver to pay for his passage. Maybe he was running. Maybe he was merely wandering. Perhaps he was just trying to get home.

"It's what's *in* the packet that has value," said Drusus, "but none to you."

"What are you going to do?" said the man fearfully, realizing that the messenger could take him forcibly to the captain, and that he clearly had the ability to do it. Drusus was a much larger and stronger man.

"I'm going to forgive you," said Drusus. "And I'm going to give you a gift." He reached into the purse on his belt and pulled out a few coins, enough to buy a week's worth of food.

"Why?" said the man, amazed.

"Because the one who wrote what is in this packet would tell me to," said Drusus.

The light grew on the horizon and the portals began to illuminate the passenger area gently. The couples near the end stirred and awakened, as did the older man in the stall next to where Drusus and the thief were. The other passengers made little noise, and Drusus became aware they were probably listening to him as he spoke softly to the man still tucked defensively into a corner but paying rapt attention to what the messenger was saying.

In a few minutes, Drusus placed his hand on the trembling man's shoulder, got up, and returned to his own stall, gathering his possessions and then going through the passageway and up the steps to the deck, to take in the brilliant sunrise. Within an hour's time the shoreline came in view, and soon they were alongside one of Miletus's many docks.

Carriages were available at the port, and after eating his first substantial meal since leaving Italy, Drusus had found a ride going his way, into the lush Lycus River valley.

4 • USA, February, 2019

After polishing Part One of my article just after Patrick met me in January, I took a break and spent the next week returning to my aborted book on theophanies and I became deeply entrenched in it. I had also developed the idea to use one of the old "harmonies of the gospels," probably John A. Broadus's version, to construct a picture book for children, illustrating as much of the New Testament as possible. I was in the thick of researching how I could reprint not just old, public domain pictures of Christ, like Sallman's or Hoffman's works, but some of the newer ones as well, like Anderson and Dewey, without having to pay royalties. I was convinced that the exceptions to copyright laws for educational purposes, especially where no sales of the work were involved, would be the ticket.

The end of the week quickly arrived and with it the return of the subject of Laodicea. I rode my motorcycle downstate to meet Patrick at his newly discovered Mexican restaurant, the

Tamal Café, which was really sort of a hole in the wall in a recently renovated downtown. It had formerly been "The City Café," a narrow room with a counter on one side that had been turned into a bar, and tables, two wide and ten deep, ending at the kitchen.

We enjoyed the signature dish, a plate of four tamales topped with chili and cheese. It reminded me of the same dish I had probably had hundreds of times in law school at a little place just off campus. I couldn't keep visions of my student self out of my head throughout the meal.

We retreated to Patrick's house after lunch and had the run of the place since his wife was making a little extra income for them as a school counselor. We settled into his plush den chairs and picked up basically where we had left off the week before.

"Here's the text of Part One," I said, plopping the pages of the article down on the table between us. "It's technically a draft, but you know me. I tend to write my first draft as my last draft, minus any typos."

"I'll read it later and proofread it, if you want," he said."

"Fine. I've caught a few things myself, but you never can proofread your own material successfully, you know."

Patrick picked up some of his own printouts that were beside him and hoisted them up into view. "I did a little more Googling after last week. Didn't come up with a great deal more than I had. Of course, I had church things to tend to."

"When are you going to retire?" I said. "You don't want to

work till you drop, you know."

"I don't know. A year more at least. I could retire now. But things are going well, and frankly I'm not sure what I would do."

"Fish twice a week. Golf twice a week. Thing is, every day is Saturday. You'll come up with something."

"I could write books, like you," he said. "But I tend to labor too long over writing. It doesn't come easily a lot of the time."

He pointed to my manuscript. "I wouldn't have been finished with Part One in a week if it had been me writing it instead of you."

"Well, I'm prolific, but that doesn't say anything about profundity." I was baiting him with self-abnegation again.

"Phooey," he said. "It's probably brimming with erudition, unlike me."

"See there," I said, 'brimming with erudition.' That's the kind of thing you'd write, and it just came trippingly off your tongue." He had baited me back.

"Okay, enough of that. Where are you on Part Two?"

"Well, where I want to go with it is to suggest the kind of thing Paul might have written to Laodicea. I want to start with the idea that the letter dictated by Christ to John in about A.D. 95 might never have been written if the Laodiceans had paid heed to what Paul wrote to them thirty or thirty-five years before."

"Interesting," he said. "But that wouldn't provide you with

a lot of material for what he might have written."

"No, and that's why I won't have much to say on that point, unfortunately. I do think, however, that you can look at some of his other letters where he was forceful about Christology and discipleship, and you can figure on maybe his echoing that kind of material in a letter to Laodicea."

"Like what?"

"Well, for instance, if the Laodiceans weren't really being serious about submission to Christ as Lord. If they were backing off on their witness, just so they could escape persecution, Paul might have given them the gospel demand like he did in Romans: confess with your mouth that *Jesus is Lord,* as well as believing in your heart in the resurrection."

"You think they were fudging on obedience, then."

"In the matter of evangelism, yes," I said, "and I'm going back to my assertion that they understood either implicitly or explicitly that evangelism was mandatory."

"But do you think that was their main problem? Not making disciples?" said Patrick.

"Well, no. I think there may have been more than that. If they were mostly responding to persecution, then they would have had to show their compliance with Roman culture in some other way."

"You mean prove they were regular guys if somebody challenged them?"

"Yeah, like if some magistrate questioned them and put

them to the test in something," I said.

"Like what?" he said.

"Like going along with the cult of the emperor in some way."

"You think they participated in temple prostitution?" Patrick said with some surprise.

"Not sure. It was prevalent. But so was eating meats recently offered as pagan sacrifices."

"As Paul made very clear, I know."

"Somebody may have made it difficult for them to avoid eating sacrificial meats without giving themselves away as Christians, or at least as *scrupulous* Christians."

"Could be," he said. "You think of anything else?"

"That's about it, other than unspecified carnal behavior. I mean, if they didn't regard Jesus as Lord of everyday life, *everything* we do, then I suppose any kind of compromise could have been taking place."

"Coffee?" said Patrick.

"Hardly a carnal compromise," I said.

"Ha ha." Patrick stepped into the kitchen and began brewing two cups with his pod-style maker, without pausing the conversation.

"But you're back to the dead end," he said. "We ain't got the letter. Certainly not the genuine letter from Paul's hand." He came back with two steaming mugs. "It's lost to the mists of Christian history."

"Hey, I like that. Can I use it?" I said.

"Credit me in a footnote."

"Ha ha." I slurped from the cup, taking in a lot of air to cool it.

"So, what are you going to say about what happened to it?" he said.

He had a couple of coffee warmers on the table between us. This was obviously where he and his wife sat in the morning to wake up their brains. I set my mug on one of the warmers and turned it on.

"Well, first off, if only briefly, I have to deal with the two spurious claims."

"Marcion's, for one," he said.

"Yeah. Who claimed he had the letter, but never produced it."

"Ever wonder what would have happened if he hadn't been denounced as a heretic by the church at the time?"

"I think we can confidently presume the church would have been shut down either during his lifetime, or shortly after his death in A.D. 160. Gone out of business. Died on the vine."

"And other metaphors," Patrick mused. "What do you think was in the letter he had? Marcion's."

"*If* he had a letter, I think he wrote it himself," I said. "And it would have had all kinds of support for his heretical views."

"That's what I've read, too, and I tend to agree. I mean, if you had it, why not produce it? At least to a small group of witnesses, even if you were concerned about protecting it from theft or something."

"But I think," I said, "that he never had one. I think he made it up."

"What about the other one?" said Patrick.

"Ah, the 4th century letter. Latin."

"Right. And what I read says there was never any Greek text for it."

"Condemned as a forgery just about as soon as it appeared."

"Who did that?" said Patrick.

"Jerome. Saint Jerome. Born middle of the 4th century. No slouch of a scholar for his day. His translations of scriptures ultimately became the Vulgate Bible."

"I had forgotten that," said Patrick.

"I'll 'fess up: I never knew that before all this study."

"So he condemned the Latin letter to Laodicea why? Because there wasn't any Greek behind it?"

"Yep. It just suddenly cropped up in Latin one day. After that, at least some of the scribes kept copying it along with the scriptures. Till at least the Reformation, anyway."

"Have you read that thing?" said Patrick. "It's all of about nineteen or twenty verses long."

"And choppy. Like cut and paste from known letters of Paul."

"Yeah. When I finally found a copy of it and read it, even in the *English* it's an obvious fake. Not that I would know one if I saw it in the Latin. But I mean, it's *bad* writing."

"Totally agree. I found myself thinking, with what little I know of Greek, if you were to translate that letter back into Greek, it would be *terrible* Greek. No way Paul could have written it."

"And your expertise in Greek is not slouchy, by the way," said Patrick.

I nodded once toward him to acknowledge the compliment and then shook my head to deny its accuracy.

"Okay," he continued, "so you're going to completely pan the two claimants to being the Laodicean letter. Then what?"

"I don't know. I'm basically finished with that, I suppose," I said. "For lack of anything substantial to say more."

"What about the question of how in the world the letter just completely disappeared?" said Patrick. "I've been thinking about that during the week. And I'm not just echoing what other people have said. In fact, I don't know that I ran into this line of reasoning anywhere else."

"What line?"

"The idea that a letter from Paul could have just *disappeared!* Look, we know that Paul's letters to the churches at Rome, Corinth, Galatia, Ephesus, Philippi—where else?—Thessalonica, Colossae, and the pastoral epistles to Timothy and Titus, they were all copied and recopied. And they were widely read, most of them in a short time after they were written. Even Philemon, which was a personal letter—well, really Timothy and Titus, too—they were copied and circulated. It's like those guys realized that while the letters were *personal*, they weren't supposed to remain *private*."

"Oh, I like that! That's a great idea. And I think I see where you're going with it," I said.

"And the reason we have his letters today," he continued, "is that all this copying started *right away*. When they got them, they copied them. I'm thinking that what Paul actually meant by telling the Colossians to swap letters with Laodicea was that they were to make a copy as *soon* as they got it, and pass along the *copy*, not just share the original."

"Which brings you back to—"

"Wait, let me finish my thought," he said. "It was the fact that *Paul wrote it* that made them realize they had to copy it. It was kind of like an ancient version of re-Tweeting or forwarding on Facebook."

"The compulsion to pass along the good stuff," I said.

"Right! Everybody knew that if Paul wrote it, it was going to be epic. It was important. So they copied it. They re-Tweeted it."

"Keep going," I said. "You're on a roll, here."

"What that means," he said, "is we probably have a good indicator of what happened to the Letter to Laodicea." He paused for a second and seemed to be waiting for me to finish his thought. I would have, but he did it himself.

"Since we don't have any copies, it's more likely that Paul

never wrote it, or that it never got to its intended addressee, rather than that it did get there but just didn't make it to the copyist's table." Patrick had sat up to make his point, and he sat back and reveled in his reasoning, looking at me for my reaction.

I was chasing a rabbit, but I decided to stick in another thought. "Would that mean that we do or don't know if he wrote any other letters than those in the New Testament?"

"What? You mean just from the absence of copies?"

"To follow your reasoning, yeah," I said.

"I think it would strongly suggest," he said, "that he didn't write any others. For instance, did he write a letter to Berea? We don't know. But simply because we don't have any copy of such a letter, I think we can reliably presume that he *didn't* write one. The mere absence of a copy of a genuine letter of Paul the Apostle suggests that he didn't write one. See?"

"That's kind of arguing from a negative," I said. "Tends to be difficult to make your case. Like proving someone is dead because they aren't around. No body usually means it's tough to prove murder."

"But in this case," he said,"we have a definite reason to argue from a negative. We have multiple examples of people copying Paul's letters. It's the sole reason the translators of the King James Version had hundreds of copies of Greek New Testament documents. The very first recipients of letters, and gospels too, had to preserve them, not just by keeping the originals safe, but by copying them. If they hadn't done either one, we wouldn't have them."

I was letting the logic sink in, and it was exciting me along several directions of thought. It was still a bit dodgy logic, but it produced at least a probability as a conclusion.

"And add to that," he continued, "that we already *know* that Paul wrote a letter to Laodicea. He said he did. He assumed it had already gotten there by the time he wrote to Colossae. So if we know he wrote one, the absence of copies leads to only one possibility. Well, okay, make that a high *probability*. If my reasoning is correct."

"Which is," I said, "that the letter wound up in the first century version of the dead letter office, or sank along with a courier on a ship, or something like that."

"Or, something more nefarious," said Patrick. "Like what you suggested last time."

I finished my coffee and turned off the warmer. Patrick's had produced evaporation rings above the descending level of coffee, as he had pursued his thoughts without drinking any brew.

"Which leaves me back at square one, in a way," I said. "Which is that the genuine letter—and we believe there was one—was, to use your phrase, 'lost to the mists of Christian history.' Huh?"

"I guess so," he agreed, trying to think if there were some avenue of thought he hadn't pursued.

"I think the bottom line for the article will have to be that in the Christian world we have what God providentially preserved."

Our hands were both behind our heads as we reclined in our chairs. After another minute or so of silence, I glanced at the clock. It was nearly four. This time it was I who had to get back home.

"When do you have to submit copy?" Patrick said.

"They want it by the end of this month for publication the first of May and the first of June," I said. "I'll have Part Two written by this time next week. Got to get all this conversation down while it's still hot."

"It was tamale inspiration."

"Probably," I said.

I left on my motorcycle, taking the long way home through the country rather than going on the Interstate, solely because I enjoyed two lane roads through the foothills. And it offered the opportunity to think.

After supper I retreated to my office and ground out the substance of Part Two. It contained everything I had brainstormed with Patrick, ending on a mysterious note:

> Most Christians assume that the letter was lost to the mists of Christian history. We believe we have the New Testament God meant us to have, and even another letter of Paul's—genuine though it was—was apparently not meant by

the Holy Spirit to be part of his written word.

Still, it makes us wonder where the letter went. Perhaps we'll never know.

I submitted both parts of the article the following week and breathed a sigh of relief.

Writing was like giving birth to a baby, I figured. My wife would probably disagree, but at least without the pain involved, it was true. The conception of an idea led to the development, which grew and grew and almost overburdened the mind until the time came to bring forth the result. The labor of writing was, for me at least, usually not done over a protracted time but in a few hours, really. And when it had come out of me into a manuscript and was delivered into the hands of the editors, I felt dramatically lighter.

Okay, it's an extended metaphor under construction.

In May the first installment of the article came out. It generated a fair amount of interest. The editor forwarded to me a couple of physical letters and a few dozen emails responding to it and expressing anticipation of what I might say in the second installment, which would probably leave devotees of arcane biblical subjects with more questions or objections than anything else. I decided in advance not to carry on any correspondence with anyone who might want to debate me or milk me for more information. I had said all I had to say, anyway, and as usual with me, I had moved on to other interests by then.

When Part Two of "The Missing Letter to Laodicea" came out in June, in spite of the fact that I knew what I had written, I eagerly looked at the published result. There's always a little thrill to see what you've written appear in print.

I revisited my decision to end the article on that note of mystery—"Perhaps we'll never know"—and I reassured myself it was the right call. Predictably, the editor would forward another hundred emails about Part Two, and some of their writers would take issue with me, insisting that we already know what happened, arguing for the genuineness of one of the discredited letters. Others would predict that before the end of time, maybe just before the Rapture, the letter would appear and would speak a message to the modern church that would be powerfully prophetic. I also anticipated that someone, probably writing anonymously, would tell me *he* had the letter himself, or that God had given him the content of the letter in a dream and he had written it down. There was one of those in every crowd.

It didn't matter. I had already decided I wasn't going to waste any time responding to comments. Project finished. On to the next thing.

But if I had known that writing this article in the first place would lead to my being sucked into a mystery spanning the church age, I might not ever have sat down to my keyboard and cranked it out.

5 • LAODICEA, A. D. 61

AKAKIOS LEFT HIS BUSINESS OFFICE after checking in at midday to see if his employees needed his decisions on any matter, and he went back to the government center where he maintained another, though smaller office, where he functioned as a clerk of some rank. After another hour or two there, he had completed the day's work, and he dismissed the remaining secretaries, locked the office, and left the building, headed for the house of Nymphas. Later in the evening, church leaders would gather briefly, and Akakios was included.

He thought back to the previous year, when he had been brought in by the elders to be part of a group of advisors on civic matters. He remembered the pun of one of the younger elders:

"I approve of Akakios," he said, "since clearly he's 'not evil.' The young man had chuckled, thinking his play on words to be novel. The others smiled with little enthusiasm, knowing it wasn't. In fact, Akakios heard some version of this attempt at humor at least once a month. Why his father had given him a name meaning "not evil," instead of something like "Agathinus," which meant simply, "good," Akakios had never figured out. If your name told people you weren't evil, it was more like suggesting that you weren't *exactly* evil but also weren't exactly good. Akakios had always been a bit sensitive about the matter, and he struggled to tell himself that it was just a name, after all.

As a member of the Council of Laodicea, designated a "free city," under the Empire, Akakios had a small part—he was hopeful it was soon to be a great part—in the city's ruling itself under a curator. Akakios himself aspired to be a magistrate, and he lived in such a way as to ingratiate himself to the powers-that-be and to the community in general, which means the secular community in this case. In consequence, though he had been attracted to the much publicized gospel of Jesus Christ, he remained thoroughly attached also to the secular system. And though he certainly made some sort of personal decision to follow The Way, and was just as certainly baptized as a believer, he didn't make any kind of converse decision to distance himself from public office or loyalty to the Empire under which his city was thriving. Nor did he think there was any necessary connection or conflict between the two.

Since becoming part of the Laodicean church, Akakios had held and shared his firm position that people shouldn't have to renounce patriotism or public service in order to follow Christ.

Unfortunately for the Christians in Laodicea and elsewhere, their times were not ideally suited for independent expression, and the Roman Empire was not the best of governments for religious freedom, as they had all found out. Akakios was sadly aware that the man he ultimately served through civil government, Emperor Nero, had already perpetrated a significant amount of persecution against religions not willing to acknowledge his lordship. He had begun to use treason laws to justify summary executions and to blame miscellaneous negative events on Christians who happened to be nearby. In this anti-Christian climate, it was not generally advisable to maintain a high profile as a believer in Christ, especially if it involved highlighting Christ as Lord and King.

For his part, Akakios was convinced a middle ground could be struck without forfeiting the favor of either the church or the state. But convincing fellow Christians they could proclaim Caesar to be lord of the land, without jeopardizing their commitment to Christ as Lord of all, was difficult.

From his Jewish friends in the Church at Laodicea Akakios heard a story related by the Apostle John, who had recently been living in Ephesus. The young John had witnessed Jesus' appearance before Pilate when the gathered Jewish mob was demanding Jesus be crucified. John heard Pilate say, "Shall I crucify your King?" And just as clearly he heard the chief priests say, "We have no king but Caesar."

Akakios's Jewish Christian friends were ashamed of their

Jerusalem brethren who had said such things, but they also knew those Judean Israelites had said, "Hail Caesar," in order to survive. The majority of Jews didn't want to be too closely associated with minority groups like the Zealots, a sort of terrorist faction of Jews who lost more than they won and threatened the delicate detente between the Jews and the Romans. The Jewish chief priests understood the dangers of promoting a prophetic view of their faith and their nation, which would of necessity feature their belief that ultimately, perhaps soon, Israel would throw off their latest conquerors and be established as God's chosen nation forever.

Akakios understood that the Jewish experience of trying to serve God and be obedient to Caesar as well was a parable for him and for every Christian, Gentiles included. The church championed the idea of the eventual reign of God through Jesus Christ over the whole world—though they disavowed any intention to make war to bring about this kingdom. In fact, it was a different kingdom they sought and preached, a kingdom of persons ruled by God *in their hearts*, exactly as Jesus had said it was. It was Akakios's view that such a kingdom posed no threat to legitimate governments. Even so, Roman emperors and other world rulers seemed blind to the distinction between political and spiritual kingdoms, or visible and invisible kings. The result was persecution.

Making his way on foot down through the inner city streets toward one of the larger residential districts where Nymphas's house was, Akakios ruminated on this matter of loyalties, as he continued to think about how to find the middle ground he sought. He recognized there was a climate of both implicit and explicit threat, which became the social atmosphere breathed by everyone. In this atmosphere, most people shouldn't require any extensive debate with themselves about how they should conduct themselves in public: they should be good citizens, loyal to the ones who ruled, whoever they were. Surely that was advisable for Christians as well as others. Akakios had made this observation one of the pillars of his case for reasonable compromise.

The other main pillar was his belief about the nature of Jesus in his risen state. Fashioning his emerging, personal theology after some whose names he had heard out of Jerusalem and Antioch, Akakios was convinced that Jesus—the man who had surfeited at a wedding and feasted with rich tax collectors and admitted he had come "eating and drinking"—wouldn't deny his followers the pleasure of enjoying the things of the world, within limits of course.

As he had been developing this theological position, Akakios had become not only a leading person in his community but also an emerging leader in his church. He was increasingly influential. As someone engaged in successful business and public service, and someone pursuing the relationships with public officials that would result in his achieving public office, he was admired by many people and his opinions on matters both secular and religious were respected. The tension of conducting the mission of the church in the political atmosphere of the day was palpable, and anyone who seemed to have a handle on both realms was consulted and listened to. Akakios was such a person. And he intended to cultivate the strength of his position continually.

Mistaken identity

Akakios finally arrived at Nymphas's home and found he was not presently there. No one answered his knock at the door. Nymphas would probably arrive soon. His wife was likely in the market streets. Akakios decided he would enjoy the shade of the spacious home's curtilage. He was waiting in the courtyard, sitting on a curved, stone bench, when a messenger arrived at the gate. The man said he had been directed to this house as being the house of Nymphas.

"It is," Akakios said to him, getting up from the bench. "What do you have?"

"A letter. It is for the church. From Paul in Rome." A look of gravity and importance was in the messenger's eyes.

Akakios's face surely reflected the surprise and anticipation that first came over him at the news that in the messenger's hand was a letter from the Apostle Paul himself. A few other churches had gotten letters and copies of them had begun to make their way around Asia. He knew the Ephesian church had a copy of the letter Paul had written to Christians in

Galatia, and the nearby Colossian church had a copy of one addressed to the Church at Thessalonica. These were larger churches. It had never occurred to Akakios that Paul might write an individual letter to the Laodicean church.

As suddenly as he registered surprise, however, he was struck with the realization that Paul's reason for writing might not be just to say Hello and pass on some generic Christian instruction. As with the Galatian church, he might be taking aim at something of which he disapproved. Something in the back of his mind became uneasy.

Nevertheless, Akakios smiled and thanked the messenger. He engaged him briefly in superficial conversation about his journey. The messenger, who gave his name as Drusus, briefly related how he had been robbed of the letter for a few hours, but then recovered it by the grace of God. They presently ran out of conversation owing mostly to the fact that Akakios was not overly gregarious and that Drusus himself was a man of few words, though well chosen ones when he did speak.

Drusus perhaps expected some hospitality to be forthcoming, but Akakios extended none, and Drusus ended an awkward silence by excusing himself saying he had already found lodging and needed to go there before dark. He wished the church well and departed.

Akakios realized the messenger thought he was Nymphas, but no matter. The letter was for the church and was not personal. He sat back on the bench and opened the goatskin packet containing parchment. The letter was three pages long. It began with the author's self-identification and some typical formalities. Akakios scanned it first, thinking any moment Nymphas would come through the gate. He was about to put the sheets quickly back in the packet when his eyes caught on words near the middle of the first page. There was his name.

Wide eyed, he read the words of Paul about him, and his face flushed with embarrassment and anger. He put the sheets back in the packet, closed it, and hurried to the gate, leaving before Nymphas could return, and going to his own house. He felt shame about taking the letter, but he could not allow Nymphas to have it. He could not allow the church to read it. He would not subject himself to public rebuke. Right now, he needed time to think. He had to decide what to do with the letter.

6 • TYCHICUS, EARLY A.D. 62

AS A YOUNG BOY, Tychicus had accompanied his father a few times on one of his many trips in and around the country bearing messages for government officials, businessmen and wealthy citizens. His father was a professional courier, and he knew his way around Italy, Greece and Asia. In fact, he had been to Spain a few times and promised to take his son at some point.

But Tychicus's father had died five years before and Tychicus, then nineteen, decided he would carry on the family business. He was doing so very profitably when he became acquainted with Paul, the celebrated and maligned Jew who had set out to eliminate Christians from Judea, Samaria and beyond, before being converted to the very faith he hated.

Tychicus was operating in Asia at the time, running a messenger route around cities in the western provinces, when he happened upon a crowd in Ephesus in the vicinity of a synagogue. People were pressing around the door and windows of the modestly sized building. He paused to listen to the speaker inside, and the rest was history. His history.

An apostolic friend

The speaker was Paul, until recently "Saul," from Tarsus. Tychicus heard him tell the story of his leading a violent campaign against followers of The Way—followers of Jesus of Nazareth—rounding up known members of the sect and bringing them before Jewish authorities for trial and, in some cases, execution. Of Paul's "before and after" testimony, he brought the before-account to a high point in his description of the stoning of a Jerusalem sect member named Stephen. Paul had looked on placidly and held the outer coats of several other Jews participating in the impromptu execution.

But then Paul described an encounter on the way to Damascus that resulted in an about-face for his life. The whole party was stopped in its tracks when Paul, in the lead, fell to the ground, looked into the sky, and began speaking to someone. Nobody else in his traveling party realized exactly what was happening: they heard a voice of some kind but didn't see anyone. But Paul had been blinded in the encounter; he had to be led to Damascus. And starting that moment he became an entirely different person. By the time Paul explained the gospel, Tychicus had maneuvered his way into the synagogue and fairly begged to be the first to profess faith in Jesus Christ.

Tychicus opened up an office of his business in Ephesus in

order to be able to stay there with the growing group of believers in The Way. However, Paul himself didn't remain in Ephesus long; he traveled back east; he had already journeyed extensively in Greece and was headed back home.

Within a year or so, however, Paul appeared back in Ephesus as he began a new tour preaching the gospel of Christ and starting Christian fellowships. During the two years that he stayed in Ephesus on that extensive trip, he and Tychicus had the opportunity to become fast friends. The upshot was that Paul enlisted Tychicus in evangelistic ministry. When Paul left Ephesus for other Asian destinations, Tychicus went with him, now officially part of the missionary team, along with a friend from the Ephesian fellowship, Trophimus, who had also become certain the Holy Spirit was calling him to the mission work.

During the next two or three years Tychicus ran his business remotely or from the road. He took on what messaging and courier work he could fit in with his new traveling ministry, leaving the rest of his business with the associates he had brought on more than a decade ago. Eventually, he figured, they would carry all the weight, and he would probably sell the business to them. Meanwhile, he was in and out of Paul's company as the mission team went to Macedonia, down into Greece, and to Corinth. Then they backtracked until coming back to Miletus and sailing east, arriving finally at Jerusalem. Tychicus dropped off in Miletus when Paul left to go to his home country.

Tychicus was in Ephesus when word came that Paul had been arrested in Jerusalem, and that after a series of escalating events he was being transported in Roman military custody to the Empire's capital. Tychicus escalated the pace of his own plans, making concrete preparations for selling his courier business to his associates, while he hurried to Rome to find Paul and do whatever he could for him.

Ironically, shortly after many of the team reassembled in Rome and began to develop strategies for reaching some other Italian cities with the gospel, Tychicus found himself a messenger again, though now with more important missives than any he had carried before.

Paul had been granted the privilege of renting a house in Rome instead of having to be confined to a jail. A single guard was assigned to his residence, and though he wasn't supposed to do it, the guard often ate meals with the Apostle. Tychicus and others, sometimes including a doctor named Luke, or a younger man named John Mark, came and went, giving reports, studying with Paul, and transmitting things to and from him—including monetary gifts from some churches.

A barely bearded young man named Onesimus appeared one day, receiving a somewhat confused, though happy, greeting from Paul, who then spent some time alone with him out of the team's hearing. Eventually, Paul introduced Onesimus to everyone, announcing that he was the newest convert to faith in Christ. He had come from the Colossian

Church, where he was a personal servant to Philemon, one of their members.

Tychicus knew Philemon from his time in Colossae, though he had never met Onesimus. Probably there was no reason he should have. He wondered if Onesimus had been sent with some sort of message for Paul, but there was no indication that he had. Over the next few days, the mystery was resolved by Onesimus's own admission that he had simply run away.

Important deliveries

Sensing that his time might be short, Paul determined to write letters to the churches at Colossae and Ephesus. One day he and Tychicus were discussing the situations in those two churches when they simultaneously blurted out the same idea: Paul's wish that Tychicus would deliver those letters, and Tychicus's volunteering to do it. A third letter was individually to Philemon, and Onesimus would go with Tychicus to deliver it: Paul was sending Onesimus back to his master, although now a changed young man.

Paul prayed and thought and prepared himself for several days and then dictated his letters in a few hours, watching as the words were written straight and true on the smooth, light parchment. When he had finished, he dismissed the team except for Luke, who tended to him briefly and then left him to sleep.

Tychicus left on a Lord's Day after worshiping with the

main Roman Christian congregation. He and Onesimus put together light packs for the journey and dressed warmly for chilly mornings and weather at sea. It would take him about three weeks to get to Colossae. He might stay overnight to rest, but then he had to deliver the letter addressed to the Ephesian church and go several places in the Asian provinces before he could return to Rome. It concerned him that he might be away from Rome when things started happening in Paul's case, which everyone on the team realistically anticipated would be negative. It wasn't a lack of faith on their part. The signs all pointed that way, however, and even the collective experience of the Holy Spirit's revelation was that Paul had finished his course.

While on shipboard Tychicus re-read the entire letter to Colossae and noted that Paul had urged the Colossians to mutually exchange letters with the Laodiceans. Tychicus didn't remember Paul's writing, or dictating, a letter to Laodicea. Of course, Tychicus hadn't been at Paul's house absolutely every day for the past year. Perhaps he wrote it before Tychicus was on scene. Surely he would have been the courier for the Laodicean letter if he had been with Paul at the time of its writing.

Anyway, if the Colossians acted promptly as asked, perhaps Tychicus would go with a delegation to Laodicea. He had friends there.

After seventeen long days, during which Tychicus and

Onesimus were bruised from cart travel and soaked from storms at sea, they were finally greeted with the familiar sight of Colossae's southern edge, the gracious homes of local farmers and lush fields full of black sheep. Within the hour they neared the home where the church met.

Oddly enough, Tychicus and Paul had not discussed specifically to whom Tychicus was to deliver the Colossian letter: the homeowner of the house where the church met would be a likely candidate, but if he were not the head elder, it might be best to inquire who was.

Tychicus asked Onesimus who the head elder, the pastor, of the church was. Onesimus didn't know. He had been a house servant of Philemon's, and not a very good one at that, he admitted, and though Philemon had given an open invitation to everyone in his household, family and servants, to go with him to worship with the Church, Onesimus had not shown any interest. Nor had he made it his business to know about the Church, or followers of The Way in general. Things had changed for him drastically now, but still, he was presently uninformed.

Tychicus took Paul's letter to Colossae from his pack and looked at it again. Nowhere in the letter had Paul addressed himself to the pastor of the church, and it occurred to Tychicus that Paul had not been in Colossae or heard from them in some time, and may not have known whom to address. Tychicus realized he didn't know, either. Paul mentioned Archippus and referred to his "ministry," but Tychicus knew Archippus and he wasn't the church's head elder.

Tychicus returned the letter to its protective goatskin sleeve and approached the house. As they neared the gate in the wall surrounding the property he could hear voices from within the house. He turned to Onesimus.

"Stay here for now. Sit behind the wall where you can't be seen from door. I'll call for you when you should get up and come."

"Why?" the young Onesimus wanted to know.

"I want to judge the right time. Do you think anyone here knows you?" said Tychicus.

"No. Maybe. I don't know."

"Then stay put."

Tychicus entered the gate and walked another ten feet to the entrance. The heavy cedar door was ajar, and he knocked at it and waited for a response. A tall, muscular man appeared and smiled broadly.

"Hello, friend, and may God bless you today," the man said. "What can we do for you?" He had a large, booming, but friendly voice that matched his somewhat meaty frame.

"And may the Lord bless you in the grace of Jesus Christ," said Tychicus, thus announcing his brotherhood with the Christians who worshiped here. "I am Tychicus."

"I thought I recognized you. I've seen you here before, though we've not met. I am Karpos. This is my house, and the worship house of the church here in Colossae—as you already know. Come in."

Tychicus stepped in as Karpos opened the door wide for him. Several other men and a few women appeared in the room beyond, apparently the others Tychicus had heard in conversation and perhaps uplifted prayer.

Noticing Tychicus's pack and traveling shoes, Karpos said, "You have come from some distance, I think."

"Perhaps farther than you think," said Tychicus.

"Ephesus?" guessed Karpos.

"Expand your reach," said Tychicus.

"Ha! My children are better at guessing games than I," said Karpos, laughing. "Perhaps you had better school me simply."

"Rome," said Tychicus.

Karpos's face lost its mirth but retained its expectant joy. "From Paul?!"

"Himself," said Tychicus. "And I have a letter for your church from him." He reached into his pack and withdrew the goatskin cover. He laid it on a lone table there in the entrance room and withdrew the pages, then presented them to Karpos.

"I noted in the letter, as you will when you read it, that brother Paul wants you here in Colossae to share this letter with the Laodicean congregation and to read the letter he sent them."

Karpos looked quizzical. "I wasn't aware that he had written them a letter." The others in the room looked equally surprised at the news.

"I go to Laodicea regularly on business," said Karpos. "My business in wool includes flocks pastured here and on stretches of land all the way to Laodicea and beyond, alongside the Lycus River. I'm there once a month at least. I eat with families in the church—I was there last week. They said nothing about a letter from Paul."

There was silence in the room for a moment while Tychicus considered this news. It added to the concern he felt while aboard ship coming here. If, as he felt was the case, Paul had written the letter a year or more ago, before Tychicus was consistently in Rome with him, then what happened to that letter? And who had been the courier—since it wasn't he?

"I don't quite understand," said Tychicus. "He clearly said he wrote one. Look—here." He pointed to a place on one of the pages and read out loud: "...Read the letter from Laodicea."

"Perhaps it hasn't arrived yet," said one of the women.

"Yes, that must be the case," chimed in Karpos. "It isn't a short journey from Rome, and despite the general safety of Roman roads..."

"I think not," said Tychicus. "I have been at Paul's side for most of the year just past, and I know of no letter he wrote to the Laodicean church in that time. I'm certain that if he wrote to them, it was a year, even a year and a half ago. Obviously, I was not the courier. I don't know who was."

One of the men said, "You don't think Paul may have

planned to write them but perhaps—I don't know how to say this—forgot that he didn't?"

"There is nothing amiss with the mind of the Apostle," stated Tychicus firmly. "He said he wrote it. He wrote it."

"Well," said Karpos, "I'll inquire next week when I'm there. Perhaps they just didn't mention it."

"That hardly seems likely, elder," offered one of the other men. "A letter from Paul would be major news."

"That it would," agreed Karpos, "but I'll ask just the same. If they haven't gotten something by next week, perhaps it would be prudent to send word back to Paul." The group nodded in agreement, and Karpos added, "Brother Tychicus, would *you* inquire about the matter when you return—you *are* returning to him, are you not?"

"Not right away, unfortunately," said Tychicus. "After delivering a letter to Ephesus, I will be there for two weeks or more, then Smyrna and Pergamum for another month or more each, before going back to Miletus to start back to Rome."

"That's unfortunate," said Karpos. "Perhaps someone in your business, Simon?" he said, looking at one of the men in the room.

"I have no shipments planned that way anytime soon," said Simon. "Most of my wares going anywhere farther than Macedonia go in the spring."

"We could simply hire a courier."

"That's actually my business," said Tychicus. "When I get

to Ephesus, I can send someone from my office there, at my own expense."

"No need to do that," said Karpos. "We'll surely find someone who has business in Rome soon. If not, we'll send a messenger from here."

"If he hasn't heard from you by the time I return to him in a few months, of course, I'll tell him," said Tychicus. "I only hope I will be able to."

The room became still. Everyone knew that Paul was awaiting a hearing before Caesar, but that the wheels of Roman justice ground more slowly as they reached the top echelons. And everyone knew that the growing governmental opposition to The Way threatened a negative outcome in Paul's case.

"Is there news you haven't told us?" said Karpos.

"No, not anything you don't already know," said Tychicus. "But the candle is burning."

"We will pray all the more," said Karpos, and the others joined in with, "We will," and "Amen."

"Well," said Karpos, "join us for a meal. It's nearly noon."

"Gladly," said Tychicus, "but one thing more. Philemon doesn't happen to be with you today, does he?"

"No," said Karpos. "Why?"

Tychicus went to the front door and called out, "You can come in, now."

A somewhat sheepish Onesimus popped up from behind the yard wall and came through the gate.

One of the women gasped slightly, recognizing Onesimus, and Karpos spoke for the group. "Young man, you should know that Philemon is very angry with you."

Onesimus started to speak, but Tychicus held out his hand to silence him.

"Onesimus ran away, it's true: straight to Paul in Rome. He told me while we were on the journey back here that when Paul was here, staying with Philemon, he paid special attention to Onesimus. The boy remembered that fondly."

Tychicus put his hand on Onesimus's shoulder. "Paul did more than give him a place to hide out in Rome," he said. "He led him to faith in Christ: Onesimus is coming back a new man."

Tychicus reached into his pack and withdrew another folder. "Paul also sent a letter for Philemon, dealing with the matter. It's between them, now."

Karpos studied Onesimus and nodded slightly, finally grinning. "So, you've come home in more than one way!" he said to the boy. Onesimus grinned, then beamed with inner joy.

One of the women, who apparently also knew Onesimus, strode to him quickly and embraced him as if he were her son. "Welcome home," she said.

"If it's good with Paul, it's good with us," said Karpos. "Young man, you join us, too. There's plenty to eat here."

Onesimus followed the group into the next room as they retreated into the house.

Momentarily, Karpos returned, went to the table, carefully inserted Paul's letter into the goatskin cover, clasped it gently to his massive chest, whispered a prayer, and disappeared back into the interior of the home, and the Church at Colossae.

7 • PASSING THE BATON, 2020

I WAS DEEP IN WORK on a book one morning when I received a call from an old friend in the state, a man my senior by a year who had himself retired, after attaining a fine reputation as a scholar and leader.

"Professor!" said my friend. —At this point, I'm going to assign the entirely fictitious name Wade Vaughn to my friend, for my convenience in telling you about our conversation.

Wade had called me Professor for years, because of my deep interest in theological studies. It was kind of like my paternal grandfather, who had been called "judge" by his close friends, even though he had never been a judge, only a lawyer. I had apparently earned the moniker of "Professor" to my friend Wade.

"Wader," I came back with a laugh. I had known Wade in college. Upon graduation, he had gone to seminary and I had gone to our university's own law school a year later. But we kept up with each other and wound up being fairly close through denominational work, he from his position in ministry, I as an involved Baptist layman. From early on, he was an up and coming leader, a man who made friends in high and important places. He wasn't simply a glad-hander but someone who established productive connections with scholars as well as movers and shakers in the religious world. Many of the friends across the state and country I knew in denominational work were people he introduced me to.

I may have pushed the limits of allowed description in writing even these things about Wade, because as the first order of business in our phone call, he elicited from me a solemn promise that I would not reveal his identity, as a condition of his telling me, and giving me, what he subsequently did. I have obscured his identity by giving him a fictitious name, and a few other facts I've just given you are deliberately misleading. In other words, not all the facts are entirely factual.

I had some trepidation about giving my word when I didn't have the slightest clue what he was about to reveal. Lawyers are used to such an expectation of privacy; it's called privileged communication. Doctors are held to similar expectations with their patients. Ministers in general may claim the sanctity of privileged communication when listening to their parishioners. But I was not my friend's lawyer, doctor or pastor and he wasn't asking me to take his confession. This was a friend-to-friend matter, but I had no idea whether it related to our common history in denominational work, our common friends, or an entirely personal matter. In any event, it wasn't *what* he was going to tell me he wanted kept secret, only *who* told me.

He wanted this vow of source-secrecy before he said even one more word. I couldn't even ask the general nature of the secretive information. He said he was sorry that he had to take that approach, but that he had decided he had to remain anonymous. And he said that if I were unable or unwilling to promise to keep his identity secret, even before hearing what it was he had to say, he would understand. I only assumed he would ask someone else to do the same thing if I refused; he didn't actually say he would.

I have been known through life as someone who can keep a secret. It has been a professional qualification. By this time in our conversation my interest was piqued and I was willing to promise solemnly that I would never tell who told me whatever I was about to be told. But I quickly added one provision, which I hoped he would accept. I asked him to assure me that he wasn't going to reveal that he was about to commit a crime. In the case of lawyers, for instance, the exception to the privileged communication rule is when a client says he's about to rob a bank or kill someone. My friend readily assured me, with a little laugh, he wasn't going to commit a crime, which I didn't really think was possible anyway, and so I repeated my promise.

"On my honor, Wade, I'll never reveal who told me—whatever it is. So help me God."

"Your honor is quite enough, your honor," said Wade.

A moment of quiet ensued on the phone, and then I said, "So what is it?"

He said, "I can't tell you on the phone, Professor. I have to tell you in person, and you have to see it."

Document hand-off

We arranged to meet at a place just about equidistant from us, which was about an hour since we were on opposite sides of the state. Presumably his choice of location, which was neutral and provided for privacy, was so that we wouldn't be seen together by anyone he knew who might put two and two together, however implausibly, and suspect that he had told me whatever it was that he wanted to distance himself from—though, logically, it was unlikely that anyone else knew about whatever it was in the first place. It seemed a bit cloak-and-dagger to me, but I went along with it. Out of an abundance of caution, I won't even say where it was we met, but the meeting took place in just a few days from the time of his call. Every day was Saturday for me, as I supposed it was for him, and I had no conflicts. In fact, I rode my motorcycle because it was a beautiful day and I hadn't been out on it since, well, the day before.

After shaking hands and exchanging the formalities of catch-up descriptions of our lives since we last saw each other (nearly fifteen years before), we sat down. We were in private. We had coffee, two tall to-go cups which Wade had brought to the meeting place apparently from somewhere nearby—the meeting place wasn't a restaurant—and he set his down alongside a leather portfolio he had brought with him. I stared at him, he stared at me, and finally he worked up to his opening statement.

"I read your articles last year about Laodicea," he said. "They were really good. What got you interested in the subject?"

"Oh, just an intellectual curiosity that came up in my Bible study," I said. "I often take off on these tangents. I have probably a dozen unfinished books on my computer consisting of just a few pages of introduction. That's as far as I got on them before I went off in some other direction. It just happens, in this case, that I finished my thought and sent it off to the magazine. It was too long for a single article, so the publisher and I agreed to divide it about 60/40."

"Have you ever wondered, if we had the original letter, if it would say anything we don't already know?" Vaughn said.

"I guess I have always supposed it wouldn't really add to anything we *need* to know," I said. "I think that was the point of the Holy Spirit's seeing to it that later on the church didn't even have the letter in hand, so they couldn't consider it for the canon of the New Testament in the fourth century."

"I agree," he said, "and I'm sure it didn't contradict anything else Paul wrote."

"You put that in an interesting way," I said. "You're *sure* it didn't."

"Very sure."

"Well, I guess my view of Paul would allow for his making a few mistakes," I said. "Like when he spouted off at the high priest and then had to eat crow when he found out who he was."

"Fair enough," Wade said.

"And," I continued, "I take the position that Paul's kicking John Mark off his mission team at Antioch was a mistake that God had to work around."

"Really?" he said with mild surprise.

"Yeah. When Luke described it, he used the word *apostanta* to describe Mark's leaving Paul. *Apostanta* means 'departed,' and that's how the King James rendered it, but almost all the newer versions render it 'deserted.' It *can* mean 'deserted,' of course, but that's an English choice of words, interpreted from the tone of the rest of the passage. In fact, the word used in Acts 13 to describe Mark's actually leaving Paul was another word entirely and it didn't have the sense of desertion."

Seeing my little digression might be counterproductive to the purpose of the meeting, I said, "Oh, don't worry, I don't have the New Testament memorized in Greek; that's just one of the little subjects I pored over recently. Anyway, my point is that Paul made mistakes, like all of us. I don't believe any of them were subjects of his teaching: I'm not saying that. The two I pointed out were actions of his, reported by others. I think we can recognize those mistakes in context. Anyway, that's my story and I'm sticking to it."

"Well, you may be right," said Wade. But the reason I'm sure the letter to Laodicea didn't contradict other scripture isn't just my respect for Paul."

"What's your other reason?" I said.

"In your article you said what scholars always say about the letter, that it 'apparently was not preserved.'"

"Apparently. Yes. Apparently not. And, I'm not a scholar."

"Ok, it's what others, who *are* scholars, say," he said, smiling. "And frankly I think you are a scholar. I always thought so. The fact that you don't teach at a college or seminary is irrelevant."

"Well, thank you," I said, "but these days, I'm just a retired judge."

"If you insist," said Vaughn. "Anyway, scholars say the letter was *apparently* lost. That's my other reason for being sure whatever Paul said in that letter didn't contradict his other, known writings."

"You think it wasn't lost?" I said.

"I believe it wasn't *just* lost. I think it was deliberately mislaid."

"Okay," I said, with the hesitation of confusion. "Is this a theory of yours, or what?"

"You can call it a theory. It's not just my theory—it didn't originate with me."

I waited a beat. "Well, I've never read it as a theory of anyone else's," I said. "Of course, I'm not familiar with all the literature that might relate to the subject. Maybe I've missed some hot debate in the theological world."

"No, no hot debate. More like a private theory passed on from one person to another through the years. Kept alive. For a long time."

"How long?" I asked.

"About 2,000 years," Wade said.

Another beat, and another. "What are you talking about," I said.

"I have it," he said quietly.

"You have what?"

"The Letter to Laodicea," he said, and he sat back, as if he had just removed a great weight from his shoulders.

Possibly a half minute elapsed between that statement and my response, while I peered at him first with a blank stare, then with slight amusement, and finally with wide-eyed disbelief.

"You have the lost letter of Paul to Laodicea." It was a statement as well as a question.

"I believe so, yes," he said, and he looked down at his portfolio. "I've brought it with me."

"What, a book, or what?"

"No, a handwritten copy," he said.

"Of the manuscript?" I said incredulously. "Of *a* manuscript— what?"

"A handwritten copy of the original Greek manuscript. And an English translation, of it," he replied.

My disbelief began to dissipate. I had images of crumbling papyri and fading uncials, but now I began to think he was just caught up in a re-emergence of one of the proposed letters, maybe by way of some Greek forgery purporting to be the text that Wycliffe had lacked—Wycliffe had a spurious Latin version from which he did an English translation. Surely my friend had not been taken in by somebody recycling old heresies.

Vaughn continued.

"The original is in hundreds of rotting pieces. But before it got that way, at one point, Erasmus had it and he was able to make a copy, which survives. I have that copy, and a translation done in 2009 by the person who had the manuscripts at that time."

He began to open the large brown portfolio, undoing its two leather straps secured by slightly mangled looking locks. "What I have came to me with underlying documents showing what happened to the original manuscript, who had it and where, ever since the first century." As he undid the straps slowly, he looked at me with a slight smile as if prompting some reaction.

I looked the way I felt, I'm sure: unbelieving, uncertain, and momentarily nonplussed.

He read my expression and stopped opening the portfolio. "I don't blame you for being skeptical. I was, too. At some level,

I still am, and that's part, or most, of the reason I'm here: I seriously don't know what to do with what I have."

There was another moment of awkward silence and stillness. The coffee was getting very cold.

"Well," I said, "I admit I don't know what to say, other than, 'Go on,' so, go on."

Wade resumed unfolding the portfolio, which opened out into three times its folded width. Then he slowly pulled out a sheaf of papers, most of them in plastic page protectors, and laid them on the table in front of us. There were yellowed and very brown papers, obviously quite old, and some very recent ones, a few photocopies and some handwritten and typed pages that looked as if they had been produced last week.

"What I have here is documents purporting to support the story that the original letter of Paul to Laodicea was intercepted, and then transmitted to someone else, who later transmitted it to someone else, and so on. To skip a lot of details for the moment, it was secreted from place to place until it recently came to me, of all people, about a year and a half ago."

For the next half hour he bent over the materials and went over the documents as he pulled them out of the stack one by one and laid them in front of me. He told me the story as he understood it, with a hint of detail about the person who had entrusted the entire file to him in 2018. Nothing he said gave away that person's identity: that person had given it to him under the same provision of secrecy of source. I asked no questions as he talked. He seemed to have rehearsed carefully what he was going to say, and I let him say it.

When he finished, he sat back up and seemed even more visibly relieved than before, and the expression on his face posed the question of what I was thinking.

"Wade, I don't know what I'm supposed to think just now," I said.

"I'm not asking for a conclusion," he said. "I know this will take a while to digest. I've spent the last year trying to digest it myself. I *think* I know what I believe, but I'm not sure. I know I said I was sure, but there's that trace of uncertainty about the whole thing."

"So, what do you *think* you believe?" I asked.

"I *think* I believe it's all true."

I sat back myself. "So, what are you going to do about it?"

"I'm going to give it all to you."

"Me."

"Look," he said quickly. "Along the way, it was transmitted to various other people for safekeeping, and from what I read in these documents it was done solemnly, each one entrusting to the next one something that just *one* other *somebody* needed to know about. I assume that a recipient here or there had misgivings and hesitation. I would understand your having that kind of response, too. But I have to do this. I know beyond shadow of doubt that I am not supposed to be the one to do something with this, or even to keep it any longer. I have to hand it off. And I want you to be the one who takes it from here. I'm asking you as solemnly as I know how, to be the next link in the chain."

"Me," I repeated. "Why me?" I said. "I'm nobody. I'm a guy who wrote an article about Laodicea, that's all."

"And that's why I became convinced you were the next one to take possession of the letter. I really think if the one who handed it off to me had just waited a year or two, he might have given it to you in the first place, if he had seen your articles—actually, there wasn't much chance of that. He's not even a Baptist. But he asked *me,* and there were no conditions, absolutely none, except his anonymity. The only thing I could say against accepting all of this from him was that I didn't know what to do with the stuff."

"Which would be my response, too," I said. "What would I do with it? And why not some serious scholar in a major university or seminary?"

"I could have done that, of course," he said. "But you wrote that article—"

"Ah, yes, the article that I now wish I hadn't written."

"But you did. And it was like a heavenly sign to me," he said. "It really was. You may have thought you wrote it because of some passing intellectual whimsy, but it was like the hand of God to me. Look, Professor, truth is, I just don't have the training or skills to do something with these documents."

"And I do?" I said.

"Frankly, yes."

"I don't have theological degree!"

"I don't either, Professor. I got a Doctor of Ministry. I took Greek but I don't really use it much and what you don't use you don't remember. I studied pastoral ministry, preaching, counseling, church administration, all the things you need to be a pastor. I'm no scholar. And you don't need a theological degree to do what needs to be done with these. You just need to be a scholar."

"And I'm *not,*" I countered.

"But you are," he argued, having become energetic in his entreaty. "Just like I said before. You have the equivalent of a degree, like the workingman's degree. You've used your self-study. Me, I have a sheepskin on the wall, but I don't begin to have the chops to do anything with this letter, these letters, all of it. I think you do. I *know* you do."

"We'll have to agree to disagree."

"Fair enough, but you need to hear me. I'm incompetent to study these documents, and I'm apprehensive—make that scared to death—to do anything with them other than pass them off to someone else. Like I said, your article was like handwriting in the sky, a message from Gabriel, a dream..."

"I get it. This is my fault. If I hadn't written that article..."

"It was *God,*" said Wade. He peered into my eyes, and after a moment it was uncomfortable. I looked down.

I didn't want to say what I was about to, but I felt I had to, so I said it in the gentlest possible tone.

"What if I just say No, Wade?"

"I wondered if you would feel that way, but I hoped you wouldn't. I hope you won't. I'd even say I pray you won't."

"But again, what would I *do* with it?"

"Whatever you think is right," said Wade. And he put the stack of papers in the portfolio, folded it up, affixed the straps, which didn't seem to engage, and shoved it slowly to the center of the table. "Whatever you think you ought to do with them."

It crossed my mind to wonder for a second if Vaughn were pulling an elaborate prank on me, but I dismissed the thought. He had always been the kind of guy who was as serious as a heart attack. He was on the level. I was just reaching for any kind of excuse to back away.

Instead of demurring or acting with excessive reluctance, for some reason I quietly reached across to the portfolio and drew it slowly over to myself. The die was therefore cast.

"No recommendation from you what to do with it?" I said.

"No. None. It's in your hands. I'm free of it. If you buried it, I wouldn't blame you. If you published it, I would understand. Though," he said, "I'll be like that guy in the old TV program, *Mission Impossible,* you know, the guy on the self-destructing tape, who said, 'the secretary will disavow any knowledge of your actions.' Well, in my case, I have no knowledge of the matter from the time we leave here. It's in your hands."

There was no point in any further pleasantries between us, other than the mutual expression of the hope that we would see each other again sometime, perhaps not as long as it had been since we last had. I think we both knew it was a requisite but empty courtesy. We had long since gone our separate ways in life, work, and retirement. We had closer friends for fellowship. The miles between us were both circumstantial and physical.

I rode back home with that mysterious, possibly precious package in my motorcycle's trunk, wondering why I had agreed to take it, and wondering even more what I would do with it, if anything. At home, without even opening it again, I put the portfolio on a bookshelf beside my desk and determined to think and pray about the matter before doing anything at all. When most of a week had gone by, I was alone one morning when I took the portfolio off the shelf and sat down in my recliner upstairs to look more closely at everything my friend had given me. Either I was the curator of documents of great antiquity for the first time in my life, or, I was the unwitting target of an elaborate hoax—one that had entrapped Wade as well as me—and the other shoe would drop as soon as I did anything at all with what I was reading. People would have a good laugh, and I would be embarrassed. On the other hand, perhaps now, looking at these aging papers, I was exactly what my friend said I was: the keeper of the secret.

A momentous decision

What happened over the course of the next week I will for years debate with myself about, ponder over, grieve over, assuage my guilt over, justify myself for, dismiss the importance of, and browbeat myself for, all at the same time and without relief.

My first reaction after reading the entire file was to close it back up and toss it on the shelf again and say out loud, "Poppycock! These things are fraudulent. Maybe old, but still fraudulent."

My second reaction, barely an hour later, was to open the portfolio again, look at the translation of the letter itself, shake my head in a combination of disbelief and "what if," and lay it aside gently for another hour, when I took it back up and read it yet again.

My third reaction was prompted by an assessment of the obvious antiquity of some of the documents, including the purported original document now in fragments. If someone faked the original, he did a masterful job. If the copy by Erasmus was faked, it was also extremely well done.

I decided to assume temporarily that the documents were all on the level. I took a week, pored over them, nearly memorizing them verbatim, visualized their transmission through the years and tried to get a feel for what each caretaker of them thought and felt. In some cases they had given clues to their thoughts in the notes they wrote. As I say, I was assuming, for the sake of argument, that the documents were not fraudulent.

When I became exhausted by this week of concentrated study, I packed up everything and shelved it again. But after another twenty-four hours, I sat down with the file, to think about a practical way of publishing everything, possibly with multiple bold and underlined disclaimers of my believing any of it. Or not believing it. I was stuck in a tar pit of ambivalence.

Then, for two days I sat around the house, mostly in the same spot, thinking about the entire matter. I tried to anticipate what the reaction would be from people in my inner circle, among my local denominational friends, among colleagues of the past who were still living, and anyone else who might get wind of it if I published the papers themselves, let alone any analysis of them.

I could see myself being lumped into the company of heretics like Marcion, or publically castigated with the ancient pronouncements of Jerome. If there ever had been a Greek text of the letter to Laodicea, surely it would have been found long before the New Testament canon was fixed. It would have been evaluated by the early church fathers, widely published and stewed over, studied, and either lauded or condemned. What kind of fool would think that the world would lap up the story that an American nobody, a retiree of no consequence and no scholar at all, had mysteriously come into possession of a Greek manuscript two millennia old, from the hand of Paul? —And since I had to keep my promise to my friend, I couldn't tell the story of who had given me the manuscript, even if I thought spreading the blame for credulity would help my case.

No, I became increasingly convinced that if I published anything at all, the response would be widespread criticism. And if I thought I was a loner with very few friends now, I could get ready to experience true isolation. No one would want to associate with me. I would be like that wild haired character on television who hosted a program about ancient aliens, promoting ridiculous ideas pasted together with an endless string of "what if's" and "could it be that's," resulting in a laughable story of impossible improbabilities.

The fear grew on me so steadily and forcefully that I finally decided I could not, would not, tell anyone what I had in my possession. *If,* in fact, the materials were really antiquities—or, in the case of many of them, only represented the hearsay testimony of antiquities—they still might have constituted a very, very old hoax. The fact that somebody a thousand years or more ago may have believed these even older documents and passed them on as truth wouldn't change the fact that they were fraudulent to begin with.

And even *if* the documents were entirely or mostly reliable, they shouldn't change anything about the gospel, about the rest of the New Testament, or about the church today—not if the original letter was from the hand of Paul. What they *would* do, without question, was ruin my reputation as a reasonable and well educated person if I let the cat out of the bag, 2,000 years late. I didn't know how much life I had left at seventy years of age, but I wanted to live it in happiness, being generally respected.

After a week of thinking it all over and not being able to come away with any conclusion other than that I would be a fool to release or publish the documents or anything about them, I came to a momentous decision, leading to an action that could not be undone. If I were not going to publish the letter and other documents, or publicize or even tell one other person about them—which would effectively publish them—there wasn't any reason to keep them. None.

I would shred the documents.

I remember the morning I went up and closed my door, to destroy materials that possibly—only possibly, though—represented suppressed information two thousand years old. I really saw no alternative.

At the last moment, I considered what would happen if I just tucked them away on my shelves or in my files. I knew very well what would happen. After my mother's death a few years ago, I dealt with her files and papers, reams of them, throwing away what were in some cases keepsakes of hers but that meant nothing to me. I even sorted through and dispensed with some things of my father's that my mother had never dealt with sixteen years after his death. If I kept this file of material about a long lost letter to Laodicea, someone, sometime, would see it. It would be my wife, or more likely my children. What would *they* think? And would they have any idea what to do with it? If I struggled with the question, they would either struggle and then tell someone and word would get out, or they would toss the file. The latter case would just be a delayed version of what I intended to do, myself, at this moment.

No, I was doing the right thing. I had to destroy it. It didn't matter, I told myself, that these documents had been secreted from one person to another over 2,000 years—*maybe.* It didn't matter that a chain of people—not *that* many, actually—had believed the information was truthful and should not be destroyed (though *they* obviously didn't want to reveal it, either). It was mine, now, and I believed I saw the folly of their having preserved it for generations—again, *if* they had. No. This stuff had to go, once and for all.

I turned my shredder on. I sat in front of it on a little stool, the papers in hand, removed from their plastic sleeves, and I listened to the sound of the grinding blades. I remained motionless for a minute, the stack on my knees. On top was a ten page summary of what all the other documents contained, written by my friend Wade Vaughn sometime during the last year. When I finally screwed my courage to the sticking place, I began feeding that summary into the slot, page by page, one at a time, and it came out below as indecipherable bits, soon to be in the landfill, to rot and disappear from human knowledge.

The blades ground away with finality.

That night, I woke covered in sweat, mercifully interrupting a dream. In a few seconds I had lost most of the details of the dream. It was full of fears of being lost, of roads diverging in yellow woods, either bleak or tempestuous destinations at their dark, shadowy ends.

Instantly, I was awake enough to connect whatever I had imagined in my sleep with what I had been doing upstairs in reality a few hours before. I crept out of bed and, to avoid disturbing my wife, padded as softly as I could out of the bedroom and up the stairs to my study. On the center of my desk was the large portfolio. I unfolded it. The documents were still there, stacked neatly in order. Only the summary document was missing. It was a few feet away in several thousand pieces.

If I had breathed since I had gotten up, I didn't remember it, but now I let out a long breath I had been holding in fear. I had not gone through with it. Everything was safe.

In fact, the ten pages I had shredded were recoverable, owing to the fact that before I did this deed, a day before, I had begun scanning the documents into PDF format, aborting the process after copying Wade's handwritten summary, because even at that point I convinced myself that I was going to destroy everything and didn't want even any digital copies to exist.

I sat there in my upper room around 3:00 a.m. and cried in relief over the aborted shredding, wondering now how I was going to proceed. Because in the last moments of shredding the summary documents, I finally realized the secret I had in my hands wasn't something I had the moral right either to keep to myself or to destroy. It had to come to light. I could take the abuse, I decided. I was something of a hermit, anyway; I could go further into hiding. Maybe sometime, even after my death, I would actually be vindicated.

Now, of course, I have revealed the secret, which no one before me had done except to one other person, in a chain of secrecy, down through two thousand years. With this book, the secret ends. The bag contains no cat anymore.

So, should you believe this story? Well, I don't have any more reason to believe what I tell you than what I was shown by my anonymous friend and the documents contained in an old portfolio. On the other hand, you don't have any less reason to believe it, either. This is the kind of thing that if you don't believe it, it's probably because you simply don't *want* to, not because you can disprove it.

8 • A MATTER OF PROVENANCE

THE EPISODE WITH THE SHREDDER sobered me.

I came very close to doing something I would have regretted, though a few hours before I was certain it was the only reasonable action. I'll never know what stopped me just short of reducing historical papers of that magnitude to chewed bits. Something did. Perhaps Someone did.

Once I sat back down with the folder and handled the letters and the notes with a newfound sense of their preciousness, however, I was able finally to get into that rational, controlled frame of mind I always had in reserve, for the study and planning that would lie ahead. I had to think very clearly and address all the relevant issues involved in going public with this ecclesiastical bombshell.

To my mind, the first and foremost issue was provenance. Where did a thing come from? Who made it or wrote it? Who bought it or stored it? How did it get here and can I know it is what somebody says it is? Wade told me the Laodicean documents showed "where the original manuscript went, who had it, and where, ever since the first century." I remembered his words exactly. He was talking about the letter's provenance.

What did I really know about its provenance? It was one thing for the documents themselves to state who wrote them and what had happened to them over two millennia, but I realized that Forgery 101 was simply to create documents that announced their own authenticity. That was kind of like the Jewish rule of court requiring the testimony of two or more witnesses. Just one wasn't much proof of anything. I had to have more than that. Didn't I?

On the other hand, if I didn't have more than that, should I just scrap the plan to publish altogether?

I thought of the number of Greek manuscripts of portions of the New Testament that were found here and there, in churches, in private papers of prelates, or in jars in the desert, for goodness sake. What kind of provenance did they have? A great many of them didn't have any more proof of origin than I had in the documents in front of me. Ancient documents tracked the transmission of a Pauline letter across centuries. That had to be worth something, even if the letter itself might be a forgery.

The age of the various letters and notes was clearly a vital consideration. I could submit a fragment of the original now in tatters to someone who could perform carbon-14 dating on it. I didn't know anyone right off—not my bailiwick. There was always the Internet, and the nearby University might be able to help. But how much would a carbon-14 dater (do you call them that?) want to know about what he was testing? Could I let him in on the secret? Perhaps I could, if he could be sworn to secrecy.

Provenance was getting to be a sticky matter. Maybe I needed to bone up on it before I tried to establish my own procedure. How did art curators establish the provenance of a painting? How did geologists know that an artifact somebody gave them was the real thing? How would I, not an expert at this subject at all, establish—to use the legal term for the standard of proof in a criminal trial, "beyond reasonable doubt"— the origin of the Letter to Laodicea as having been what it said? How would I lay out the evidence so that no one could doubt the genuineness of the Laodicean documents, because the evidence is beyond contradiction?

It occurred to me that not too long ago I had dealt daily with this very matter of establishing the credibility of evidence. Why hadn't I thought of that before? Perhaps because I was not in court anymore. But whatever else I might be able to do through science or scholarship, I had to approach the documents as evidence. That meant applying the *rules* of evidence.

I opened a new document in WordPerfect on my laptop and began making notes. First, I typed, "Authenticating the Evidence." The first thing that came to mind under this heading was, "Sworn statements." I didn't have any. Each of those persons who had handled the letter and the accruing set of documents with it had written clear statements of what he did with everything, from whom he had received the letter, etc., and to whom he gave it. But no one had sworn to anything.

I realized it wouldn't have mattered much if any of them had. This wasn't a matter that came before a court and carried the possibility of perjury for sworn, but false, testimony.

Was there a possibility that the letter itself, or Erasmus's copy of it, could be taken as self-authenticating—known to have been produced by disinterested sources, often in the course of regular business procedures? I thought not.

If a radiometric dating technique could establish that the unreadable original document was in fact a first century production, that would certainly help. Textual scholars might be able to render an opinion that the writing was almost certainly that of Paul—vocabulary, phraseology, subject matter, etc., were all vital. At the appropriate point, I might need to call in a scholar as well as a dater (there's that word again).

Reliability of the evidence

In the U.S. —I can't speak for banana republics—a case before any judge is proved by the introduction of reliable evidence, which is then subject to cross examination to test that reliability. The decision as to whether the burden of proof has been met is in the hands of the judge or jury. The rules of evidence are the most detailed of all court rules. There were several rules that seemed most applicable to me at the moment. I made summary notes about each in the word processing document:

ALL RELEVANT EVIDENCE is admissible except as otherwise provided by law, but irrelevant evidence is not admissible, and it may be rendered irrelevant by numerous means, including a claim that someone's character alone proves or disproves claims about him. I thought of this rule because of the involvement of someone whom one of the transmission notes described as a person of questionable character.

A COMPETENT WITNESS is someone having personal knowledge of the matter he testifies to. I thought about the competency of Erasmus to adjudge the genuineness of the original letter, which he copied in order to preserve it. Of course, there was the more tricky matter of whether it could be proven that the document purporting to be by the hand of Erasmus was, indeed, what it said. I kept running into that obstacle.

EXPERT OPINION as testimony may be offered by someone who qualifies by knowledge, skill, experience, training or education, to give that opinion. If I went the route of radiometric dating, I hoped the results would be powerful evidence for the letter's authenticity, and a scholar in ancient Greek texts would add significant weight, as well.

And then the major challenge:

HEARSAY is a statement attributed to someone other than the one testifying, offered in evidence to prove the truth of the matter asserted. For example, a witness can testify to what Joe *did*, but simply reporting what Joe *said* is usually hearsay. Hearsay is inadmissible, with various exceptions. Here was the bugaboo. I sat and looked at the documents, which I had spread out somewhat before me on a folding table. I realized that if I wanted to be technical about it, if I wanted to apply the most rigorous standard without any leeway for circumstance, everything that had come out of that portfolio was hearsay evidence. If somebody brought it before me in a court case, and the other side objected on the grounds of hearsay, how would I rule?

In fact, in publishing these hearsay documents, my *own* reporting would be hearsay, making the resulting publication hearsay *within* hearsay. Double bugaboo. But it is what it is.

Possibly I could argue—I'd probably have to devote a page or two to this—that the testimony (other than mine) comes from sources that all might be considered to fall under one of the exceptions to the legal hearsay rule: the unavailability of the declarant. The original witnesses to these notational manuscripts are all dead. They aren't here to tell their own stories; we have only what they wrote. We should consider it as valid evidence, which people should look at and consider, even if they ultimately think the dead declarants were lying or were mistaken.

But I was troubled in no small way by this problem of hearsay. The general public doesn't apply—perhaps wouldn't even know *how* to apply—court rules of evidence to the matter of the provenance of something. I had no idea how long it would be before I had something publishable, but when I did, anyone who read what I wrote about the Letter to Laodicea would need to have more than a basic commitment to evaluating the evidence for himself or herself.

Consequently, I myself had to be reasonable about forming a firm opinion that the documents were genuine. I couldn't be construed as having been swept along in the excitement of a mystery while ignoring fundamental problems with the evidence. I did not want to be seen as attempting to foist upon the world a story I should have known to be a hoax. The evidence for the provenance had to be there, and had to be convincing.

It was, as I said, a sticky matter.

A thesis

I decided to begin with a simple summary statement and go from there. What did I have in my hands? I had an original letter, now in shreds from age and fungal rot. I had transmission notes (which is what I had decided to call the notational manuscripts by the men who had stored or hidden the letter and/or delivered it to someone else). There were numerous pages of these. I had a copy of the letter by Erasmus in pretty good shape. And I had notes by two Englishmen and two Americans, who had written more than the previous caretakers of the letter. Taken altogether, this packet of papers told a story. What was it, in a nutshell? I composed a thesis sentence for whatever it was I would publish (I was leaning toward a book):

> **This is an account of a letter written in the first century by Paul the Apostle, addressed to the Church at Laodicea, received by someone at the church, but which was never read to the congregation, and which disappeared upon receipt.**

That would be my thesis. Everything I would write would be aimed at substantiating the claims involved in that basic statement.

But I wondered if I should just ask the question, Is the letter genuine, without taking a position. Then I could spend the remaining presentation in a kind of forensic debate with my readers, first arguing one side and then the other. Then the reader could form his own opinion. I finally realized that approach would be a cop out. I was sitting here looking at these documents and knowing to the bottom of my soul they were genuine. Would I consider pretending I didn't know and avoid taking a position? That was cowardice. True, just hours before,

I had tried to convince myself the whole matter was poppycock, but I finally admitted I had been fighting against the much deeper conviction it was anything but.

No, I had to take the position I had just written in my thesis statement, and then do my best to prove that thesis true by arguing that the provenance of the letter was established by the evidence.

Whether the provenance were sufficient for its acceptance as genuine would be up to the judge or jury—primarily Christians and their churches and schools—to determine. I thought to myself that it would be entirely unlikely that, even if my thesis were believed, a shockwave would ensue in the Christian world by its publication. The world outside the church would feel no vibration at all. So, I shouldn't worry myself too much if I actually convinced any great number of people with my arguments.

I also realized that after all the work I would have to do to establish the letter's provenance, most people's evaluation of my case about the letter would be based on a much simpler standard. It was the standard that, when I was a judge and presided over a jury trial, I had to try to teach a jury of twelve people, who were neither judges nor even lawyers. I had about five minutes before they retired to render a verdict, to give them an entire course in how to be a judge. I always made a little speech, with the same words every time. In the heart of that speech were two sentences burned into my memory:

> **You are to use those faculties of common sense all human beings use to evaluate the credibility of what they hear and see. Give the testimony of the witness the weight and credit you believe it is fairly entitled to receive.**

Ultimately, people would decide for themselves if Paul had written to Laodicea, if the letter had been intercepted, if it had been stowed away somewhere, if it had been passed down through the centuries, and if the crumbling bits of parchment I had in my possession were, in fact, that letter.

9 • KARPOS, A.D. 62

THE MEAL SHARED at the round table in a large inner room of Karpos's spacious house was enough for midday but not too much to ruin a generous supper when everyone there would be back in his or her own home. Karpos's wife Adoni had prepared a stew of meat and various vegetables thickened with a bit of flour and served it in a broad but shallow bowl for dipping bread. She had also reconstituted some of the grape paste from the lately ended season and poured each of her noontime guests a cup of *oinos*. Tychicus and Onesimus sat next to each other and joined in both the meal and the conversation.

"You say you have been at Paul's side constantly," said Karpos to Tychicus.

"For the past year, anyway, most of the time," said Tychicus.

"But he never mentioned writing to Laodicea," continued Karpos.

"No, never."

"Hmm. Well, as I say, I'll ask about it. But you might be

interested in knowing what the letter might have been about."

Tychicus swallowed and then turned his body and his whole attention to Karpos.

"What is it? Did they send him a question by courier, or what?"

Karpos dipped another piece of bread and half finished it, and then answered. "Well, I'm just guessing—which," and he laughed, "I've already told you I'm not very good at! But this comes from knowing people over there and having actually been with them on occasion over the past two years, ever since I bought the former Theodoros land on the riverbank and moved some of my flocks there.

"I caught wind of something going on that didn't quite seem right to me. People wouldn't talk about it much to someone outside their fellowship, even someone like me, sort of a regular visitor."

"Did you get a general idea, though?" said Tychicus.

"Yes. It seemed to be a belief about our Lord. I got the idea that they were having a sort of debate with themselves, on a continuing kind of basis, about how much it really mattered to Christ in heaven what his followers down here did day to day—as long as they didn't kill each other!" This last part Karpos delivered lightheartedly, and it brought chuckles around the table.

"I take it not everyone agreed with this idea," said Tychicus.

"Well, as I say, I didn't get a good summary of what was

going on. But I suppose there was debate precisely because there were some who did hold this view and some who didn't."

"Any problems in the fellowship, any rift, because of it?" Tychicus said. He had stopped eating. His mounting concern was now evident in his voice.

"Don't know. Maybe. Low level sort of thing. I didn't feel there was any bad blood between the people I was with."

"Could you have been with only one faction, though—heard only one side of it?"

"At times I was with a small group, yes," said Karpos, "but even when I was with the whole church, I didn't get the feeling there was any distance between people. By the way, if you ever worshiped with them, you would remember it: my, how they sing! They have people who play instruments—David's very progeny. And loud? If they have to tone it down over there to be safe, they're going to have to have a talk with a couple of their women, I can tell you!"

"Just don't you try that over here," said Adoni, lifting an eyebrow in affectionate warning.

"No, love, never," said Karpos. "Good stew, by the way."

Everyone nodded and gave their "Mm hmm," in assent.

After the meal the rest of the group left for their homes or businesses. Tychicus followed the last of them to the front door.

"I need to go to Philemon's home, now," said Tychicus. The one page letter I have for him has to go with Onesimus, or I'd send the boy back to Philemon by himself."

"Understood. You're going to be here a day or two?" said Karpos.

"No, I thought I might stay overnight, but really I need to go on to Ephesus, and I can probably still find a carriage at this hour and get about halfway there before nightfall."

"Unless Philemon delays you."

"No, I intend to deliver the letter and tell him the rest is between him and Onesimus, and the spirit of Paul."

"Ah, yes," said Karpos. "The man has a way of being here even when he isn't. You've felt that, I'm sure."

"I feel it now," said Tychicus. "That's why I need to go while there's half the day left."

"Thank you, my friend," said Karpos. "It's been good to see you, if only for an hour. When you do get back to Rome at last, I hope you'll find brother Paul well. Please tell him we pray for him every day."

"I will." They embraced briefly, clapped each other on the back, and Tychicus parted with Onesimus in tow.

Karpos went back into his home and back to the inner room where they had eaten. On a side table was the letter from Paul. Tychicus had left the goatskin cover to protect it. Karpos removed the letter and found the place Tychicus had pointed to. "**ΚΑΙ ΤΗΝ ΕΚ ΛΑΟΔΙΚΑΙΑϹ ΙΝΑ ΚΑΙ ΥΜΕΙϹ ΑΝΑΓΝΩΤΕ**," he read. [...and the one from Laodicea that also you may read.] That was certainly clear. "They should read ours, we should read theirs," he said to himself out loud.

"Adoni, my dear," Karpos called out as he went back further in the house. "I must go to Laodicea tomorrow morning."

Shortly after dawn the next day Karpos sat with Adoni eating bread and butter and munching on a few figs.

"I'll be back tomorrow. I'm going to check in with Philander. We lost a few sheep on his watch over the summer. When I've finished with him, I—"

"Well," interrupted Adoni, "That sounds rather final." She smiled.

"Not unless it comes to that," said Karpos. "Anyway, when *we're done,* I'll go over to Nymphas's house and ask about the letter."

"Will you take the letter we've just received?"

"No. We'll wait for another time. I'll have to at least mention getting it yesterday, because that's the only way we could have learned about the one Paul wrote to them, but I won't take it."

"Are you taking the horse?" she said.

"Yes. I don't have anything but a small pack. And I'll stay where I usually do." Karpos had an office in Laodicea where his men in that city worked, buying and selling, a day or two a week. The small building included a back room Karpos had outfitted with a bed and a few comforts.

"I should be going." He kissed Adoni and started around the back for his horse, in a connected stable.

"Don't let Kratos throw you again" called Adoni.

"I told you that never happened!" he said. "I fell, that's all."

"Well, don't fall, then."

"I love you, my dear."

"I know you do. And what would you do without me?"

"Work myself to an early grave, and become thinner."

Karpos put his bag on Kratos's back and mounted. The seven or eight miles from Colossae to Laodicea would take only a while.

At the edge of Laodicea Karpos steered Kratos right and they went around the town and to the northeastern edge, alongside thc river. His little office house was conveniently nestled in the perimeter of town with its back windows overlooking his newest pasture.

No one was in the office as he left his personal items and then headed toward Nymphas's home. If Philander wasn't working, Karpos wouldn't go to see him at his house on business. He would wait until morning, on his way out of Laodicea and back to Colossae.

Nymphas's spacious and gracious home was only a bit larger than Karpos's, but it was on a wonderfully wide street. The afternoon was half over and Karpos wondered briefly if Nymphas had even finished work for the day, but when he came within sight of the house, he saw the head elder in his yard, pruning some branches out front that had made too low a canopy over a bench.

"Oh, good," said Karpos as he rode up to the gate. "You

were expecting me."

"Karpos! Good to see you," said Nymphas. "Yes, I baked bread. Nikippa did, anyway. Come have some."

Karpos dismounted, tied Kratos to the front gate, and followed Nymphas into the house. They grasped each other's arms in greeting at the front door.

After a cup of water, a bite of bread and a few trivial remarks by each, Karpos waded into the matter he had come about.

"Tychicus came to my home yesterday."

"Did he! How is he?"

"He is well. It wasn't a social visit; he was there on business and he's likely in Ephesus by now. He came to drop off a letter."

"I take it that it wasn't just a letter," said Nymphas.

"No. It was more. It was a letter from Paul for our church."

"Paul!?" said Nymphas. "Is he still…" Nymphas didn't finish the thought but turned it into something else. "Is he still—in Rome?"

"No need to be afraid to say it," said Karpos. "Is he still alive? Yes. Still in his rented house. Still wooing his guard to accept the gospel. Still teaching remotely."

"What does the letter say?" asked Nymphas.

"I actually haven't read it all yet," said Karpos. "I wanted to be with the other elders when we all read it for the first time."

"Good idea."

"But Tychicus did point out one thing to me. It's a place

where Paul wrote that your church should read our letter and our church should read yours."

"Ours?"

"Yes. Your letter from Paul."

"There must be some mistake. Paul hasn't written us a letter. I would to God that he would. We need all the teaching we can get from the apostles."

"I think the letters that are being written these days are going to be our own scriptures eventually. The right leg, where the left leg is the law and the prophets."

"We have a copy of Mark's—more than a letter. It's a book, practically. His gospel account?"

"We hope to have one soon," said Karpos. "I've written to Jerusalem about it. I even offered to pay a scribe to copy it."

"Back to this letter," said Nymphas. "It said *we* have a letter from him?"

"Yes. And you're saying you don't?" said Karpos. "Even just a short note?"

"No, nothing. When was it supposed to have been written?"

"That's the thing," said Karpos, "Tychicus said he is quite sure Paul didn't write it during at least the past year, perhaps a year and a half, because he has been with Paul most of the time during this year and Paul didn't write it during that time. He hasn't even mentioned it."

"So Tychicus wasn't sent to deliver it?"

"Obviously not. Paul must have had someone not associated

with his team in Rome to bring it here. I'm thinking it would have been someone who came from this region."

"If he wrote it a year ago," said Nymphas, "it would have been here about eleven months ago. Unless the courier had other stops to make first. But a year's delay seems unreasonable, even for the laziest couriers."

Karpos nodded. "I told Tychicus I was here last week and that no one mentioned a letter from Paul. I thought certain that if you had gotten one, the brothers here would be talking about it."

"For certain!" said Nymphas. "But—and I hate to bring this up—are you sure Paul hasn't become forgetful?"

"Tychicus assures me that the lights in Paul's house are all lit."

"Then we must find out what happened to the letter," said Nymphas. He made a fist and gently rapped it once on the table.

Karpos said, "Tychicus said he would have one of his messengers go if we didn't find out in a few weeks, but I said we would take care of it. At the moment I was thinking our elders—really just I—would inquire privately without letting you know; I felt it would set you up for needless disappointment. But finally, I realized this really should be our business together, since we were to share letters. I knew you would want to send a message by courier as soon as possible."

"We will. I'll bring the matter up before the two other elders two days from now, and we'll gladly hire a courier."

Karpos nodded and the two sipped and munched and nursed their own thoughts.

"What will we do if Paul assures us he wrote to you, and tells us when?" said Karpos.

"We'll hunt down the courier who brought it and get to the bottom of this," said Nymphas. "We can't afford to let something written by the Apostle to the Gentiles just disappear into thin air." Nymphas was genuinely upset.

"What do you suppose it said?" asked Karpos. "Or *says*—we have to presume it exists *somewhere.*"

Nymphas paused a few seconds, picked up his cup and readied a drink, and then said with what seemed to Karpos like artificially adopted nonchalance, "No idea."

Karpos watched him, and believed Nymphas was guarding his response.

"Well," said Karpos. "We'll find out, *eventually*, I suppose."

"Meanwhile," said Nymphas, "Do you want to let us read what he wrote to you? —After you read it and pore over it, of course."

"Yes, certainly," said Karpos. "But before we bring it to you, I'm going to have a scribe copy it, at least once. Others will want to read it, too."

"Good idea," said Nymphas.

The two sat back and enjoyed the cool-ish day a few moments, in relative silence.

“Everything still going well here with the church?” said Karpos.

“Yes, yes,” said Nymphas. “We could do with a bit of divine instruction on a few things—now and then, you know. Couldn’t we all?”

“True, true,” said Karpos.

After a few minutes more, Karpos decided not to pry any further, and he made his excuses and left, going to his little office for the night.

10 • CARETAKERS IN ANTIOCH

ILLYUS HAD A PROBLEM. As one of Akakios's best though distant friends, he would have trouble refusing his request, and he had plenty of misgivings about acceding to it. He sought a way to mitigate the possible personal impact of accommodating his friend, but it would have to be something he couldn't tell Akakios was a condition of the bargain.

It was late in the 8th year of the reign of Nero Claudius Caesar Augustus Germanicus. A courier bearing numerous letters from points east to Antioch of Syria and other regional cities—Tarsus, Aleppo, Damascus—came to Illyus's magisterial office near the center of the city. The personal note had been included in an official message to Illyus, who had been friends with Akakios since official business brought them together in Tarsus a decade before.

The message to Illyus said Akakios would be arriving in Antioch in a week's time to see him. Akakios hoped Illyus would provide accommodations for the night, before he left again at first light. Illyus lived in a spacious home on Antioch's western edge. When the Church of Antioch had formed twenty-five years or so before, the growing assembly had met in his house, until they switched to an even more spacious building in the southern part of the city.

Illyus was a well-regarded leader in Antioch. He was also one of the church's deacons. Among other things he kept and cared for the congregation's library of documents—papyri and parchments containing copies of scriptures, other letters and papers relating to the church, and miscellaneous records the church thought worth keeping for spiritual purposes, for posterity or for official information. Akakios had not said in his brief letter the week before what his visit pertained to, and Illyus wondered what it could be about. He was aware that Akakios considered him a friend, but Illyus had been wary whenever he had been around Akakios. Akakios had occasionally sought to hitch his wagon to a star, but Illyus never reciprocally dropped Akakios's name in conversation.

Akakios arrived midday precisely a week later. He had a personal assistant with him and a team of hired men who handled their carriage and horses. Upon his introduction at the government offices of Magistrate Illyus he was shown in to see his friend. They caught up on personal and family news since last they had seen each other, about a year previous, and then sat on either side of Illyus's cedar desk. Akakios brought out a leather pouch, sealed with his personal seal, and set it on the desk between them.

"This is something I need to entrust to you," Akakios said. "I have no one else I trust more, and most people I would trust too little to keep it."

Illyus had a look of almost amused curiosity on his face. "What is it?"

"I cannot tell you," said Akakios. "That is why it is sealed. I require your trust precisely because of the contents. But nothing in the contents relates to you. I only ask you to be their caretaker temporarily. They need to remain entirely private, known only to me."

Almost conspiratorially Akakios added, "I cannot trust my household to respect my privacy in this matter, for reasons I will not discuss out of courtesy to them. But I have sensed for the few years we have been friends that you are a man who can be trusted with a confidence."

"As should any man of government or leadership be, in the public or in the church," said Illyus. "Still, it's a curious request."

"I realize that it is," said Akakios, "but a request I must make of you. What I hope is that you will secure this pouch along with other documents in your keeping, documents to which you, and only you, have access."

"If it is related to government," said Illyus, "I could keep it here with my magisterial papers and books."

"Oh, no, my friend," said Akakios, "I should think that

would render it vulnerable."

"Very well. I will take care of whatever this is, until you return for it."

"I don't know when that will be," said Akakios.

"No matter," said Illyus. "I will have it."

"Either I or someone I authorize may return for it in—well, some time in the future," said Akakios.

"Very well," said Illyus.

The rest of their conversation was about their governmental aspirations, the regional appointees they knew in common, and news and rumors circulating about goings on in the Empire, and the general progress of their respective churches. They shortly left the government building together, Illyus carrying the leather pouch. They went to Illyus's home, where they dined comfortably. As he had said, Akakios left early in the morning for the several days of travel back home to Laodicea.

Before going into the center of the city to conduct his day's business, Illyus tucked the leather pouch into a cabinet where he was certain it would be secure. But all day he thought about the entire matter and by the time he returned home at day's end he had decided what he would do.

He decided to write a document to keep with the leather pouch, whatever was in it. What Illyus wrote, if it was copied verbatim by caretaker(s) along the way,[1] began: "The circumstances surrounding the enclosed, sealed pouch, the contents of which are unknown to me, and the manner in which I received it, are troubling to me."

Illyus then wrote at length several details about his reaction to the meeting, about his acquaintance, Akakios, and about what he suspected the pouch contained. He hated to be have been put in a position like this, and he could have avoided it by refusing—he would have said, "politely declining"—to accept the secretive pouch. He stated in his note, however, that he firmly intended to keep his pledge to his friend to keep the seal on the pouch sacred, and its contents secret.

When he returned to his house, Illyus retrieved the pouch and placed it and the freshly written paper—scribed in Greek, still the language of business in the region—in a still larger, reinforced leather pouch. He then closed that pouch, took a flat leather strap long enough to wrap around it, tied up the entire packet, and dripped sealing wax on the knot. He then wrote on the flat side of the strap stretched tightly across the outer pouch:

> Contents under strict and legal seal. Do not open. This pouch will be reclaimed by a party identifying himself as

---

[1] The document ascribed to Illyus as received in 2020 appeared most certainly to be a copy made somewhere along the way, perhaps by Erasmus.

authorized to do so.

He did not say that Akakios would return for it; while Akakios hadn't asked him not to reveal who gave him the pouch, Illyus did not want Akakios's name on the outer pouch, even though he named him in his own notes included along with the smaller pouch inside.

The two-page writing he enclosed expressed his misgivings about taking charge of the pouch when he didn't know its contents, and it explained how he came into possession of it. He described what he knew of Akakios, that he was more a professional acquaintance than a friend, and that he was a leader in the Laodicean church. Illyus said he knew by reputation that Akakios was a social and political climber, and that contacts in the Lycus Valley region reported that Akakios was a leading proponent of a belief that Christians had, on the whole, been too insistent on a code of conduct that reflected the Mosaic law, and that they should declare themselves to be free in Christ, presumably to do as they pleased. Specifically, Akakios had spoken to numerous people about his admiration of a certain Nicolas, a claimant to being a follower of The Way, but who had espoused a path of discipleship that could include guiltless celebrations of the traditional, regional religions, which included temple prostitution and feasts dedicated to pagan gods.

Over the decade Illyus had known Akakios, he had engaged

in conversations with Christians traveling through the region, and he had run into a number of them who had heard the name of Akakios in connection with a disturbing trend in beliefs prevalent in the entire Lycus Valley, including Colossae and Hierapolis. The consensus was that Akakios was a leading proponent of a view of Jesus that saw him as a spiritual guide, a heavenly king, but not thoroughly concerned with every action of his disciples on earth.

Illyus wrote about Akakios without wholesale speculation, but he could not be honest without expressing his deep concern about Akakios's beliefs and influence on the church at Laodicea. And to the point, he wrote that he strongly sensed that what was inside the leather pouch Akakios brought him had something to do with the vague sense of ferment developing in the Laodicean church. He assured whoever read his notes that he had not betrayed Akakios's trust, but he also said that in storing the pouch as he had, he hoped the reader of the notes would be someone many years from now, when whatever the pouch contained had no power to harm anyone.

When he finished writing his notes and sealing them and the secret pouch under even more leather, he tucked the larger package back where he had kept the smaller one overnight. The next Lord's day—as he had actually said in his note he would do—he carried the secretive leather pouch with him to the meeting of the Church at Antioch, planning to store it in a safe enclosure among the church's scriptures, letters, and other records. If Akakios himself returned for the inner pouch just a month, two months, or a year later, Illyus told himself he would go get the pouch, discard his notes, and give Akakios his sealed original. But if anyone else came for it, Illyus determined he would give that person the entire packet, and be done with Akakios.

The large pouch, containing the small, sealed pouch and Illyus's notes was tucked away in a musty corner with other documents. There it remained, untouched, through Illyus's lifetime.

And there it stayed, moved only short distances to other rooms in other buildings, and then only in stacks of aging records, through the lifetimes of generations of librarians in the Church at Antioch for a thousand years.

11 • Basil

For several centuries prior to the year 1054, the Western and Eastern Churches grew further apart over theological and ecclesiastical differences, for various reasons including their conflict at the very top: Western Churches accepted the primacy of the Bishop of Rome: the Pope. The Eastern Churches believed in the equality of the authority of all their bishops, with the patriarch of Constantinople being only "first among equals."

There were other points of conflict. There was a vast and growing divide between political entities in Europe and Asia. And, of course, there was the language difference in the church: Latin in the West and Greek in the East. Add the much argued difference over ikons, and an official split between East and West was inevitable. In 1054, in what became known as the Great Schism, which involved mutual excommunications, the Western Church came to be the Roman Catholic Church and the Eastern became the Orthodox

Catholic Church.

Not everyone in East and West wanted the split to take place. No doubt there were hundreds of church leaders in East and West, and untold thousands of members, who knew people across the dividing line, who had family or friends in churches on the other side—geographically as well as theologically. In Poland and Hungary, the Western Church dominated while in the Eastern Slavic principalities and the Byzantine Empire the Eastern Church dominated. In fact, Italy itself was divided, with portions of the "boot" of the country having mostly Eastern—what would become Orthodox—churches, like those in Greece just a few miles across the Adriatic Sea. As travel and commerce continued to build connections between geographic areas, conflict about church matters provoked taking sides, but it also generated attempts at compromise.

Among those church leaders who had developed networks of friendship that included the other side of the widening ecclesiastical divide was Basil, a deacon in the Syriac Orthodox Church, which included the congregation in Antioch. Basil had traveled extensively as a younger man and had church colleagues in Rome, Venice, Athens, and Constantinople among other places. At home in Antioch, he was officially charged with the duty of keeping the extensive, and ancient, library of the entire, regional church. Many volumes among the older scrolls and parchments, in particular, had been undisturbed in many, many years. Some of them had been kept in shuttered shelves and cabinets. The sheer number of them discouraged organization, and many librarians through the years had done the minimum in organization, as dust became thick in the dark recesses of the library's rooms.

Basil was a man of a different sort. When he looked at the many hundreds of volumes, he wanted to know, and he wanted anyone else to be able to know, just what the church had. The ancient and historic tragedy of the destruction of the library at Alexandria, Egypt, was a bit of history every librarian whether religious or secular knew. Every one of them protected his collection, whether a hundred or ten thousand volumes, from fire and flood and theft. But sometimes, they took too little care organizing and cataloguing. Basil was determined to change the bad habits of several hundred years of previous caretakers of the church's library.

Early in A.D. 1049, he set to work going through everything, absolutely everything in the library, counting the volumes, sometimes assigning titles to untitled works, organizing them by narrowly defined subjects and cataloguing them so as to be able to locate them easily. The oldest volumes, which had been kept in the dry in fairly secure fashion, included several leather and vellum packets. Most of these packets were easily opened. One of them, however, was mysteriously sealed. It had Koine Greek writing on a leather strap tied around it. There were differences between the street Greek of a millennium earlier and the dialect Basil read and spoke—and the writing was in uncials, which made things a bit more difficult—but it was still Greek and he could make sense of it. It said the contents were under legal seal and would be reclaimed by some authorized person.

There was no way for Basil to know how long the pouch had been in the library. He believed the library had absorbed smaller libraries from much earlier, even back to the first century, but he couldn't determine if this volume was that old, or if it had been placed in the Syriac Orthodox Church's library sometime in the eighth or ninth century. Nothing on the leather pouch indicated who wrote what was inside—if, in fact, there were anything inside that was writing. It was in the library, after all, but it didn't appear ever to have been opened, and Basil didn't know what it contained.

The previous librarian had died suddenly in the Year of Our Lord 1030, and Basil had been appointed to take his place. His predecessor had given him no instructions about the library, because he didn't know he was about to die and didn't know who would succeed him. Basil came to the job with no warning and no preparation.

So, as he looked at the old volumes, many of which had uncertain histories, he opened and looked at each of them to attempt to categorize and list them. When he came to the old leather pouch, he had a decision to make. While he didn't know just how old the pouch was, he was certain it was more than two generations old, owing in part to the old Greek dialect on the strap. He suspected it was as old as five hundred years, at least. Clearly the "authorized person" mentioned on the strap was not coming for it. He thought it unreasonable to assume that a succession of "authorized persons" had been provided for over several centuries, none of whom, obviously, had come to retrieve the pouch. The most logical conclusion was that the person who filled and sealed that pouch was the only authorized person who could have reclaimed it, or that possibly only one other person, an assistant of the one who sealed the pouch, was authorized at the time, but that both of them were long dead. Perhaps very long.

Basil was the librarian. No one person, anymore anyway, owned anything in the library of the Syriac Orthodox Church; all of it belonged to the church itself. Basil believed that fact gave him the authority to look at any and every document in the course of his work. He needed to know what was in that leather container.

Basil would later write about the moment. He closed the door to the library, even though he didn't know of anyone else in that part of the building at the moment. Then he laid the leather pouch on his main table. He inspected the knot, still permeated with sealing wax, filthy with embedded dust and grime. He pulled at the leather gently, and it broke right at the knot. In fact, the leather was more brittle overall than he had thought it to be, and in opening it slowly he still broke it apart in the crease along a third of its length. When he had the flap flat and the opening exposed, he gently reached in and felt for the contents. The pouch contained another, smaller leather pouch, and several sheets of parchment with it. He was able to remove the smaller pouch with its accompanying papers, which had stuck to it somewhat. The papers seemed to be explanatory notes relating to whatever was sealed in the inner pouch.

Basil was able to separate them carefully. Before reading them, he would open everything and see what he had. He inspected the inner pouch, the flap of which was sealed to its side with wax, which was brittle and cracked, but still barely intact. A gentle pull dislodged the crusty seal and the pouch came open. Looking inside, Basil could see it contained only three pages of parchment. Separating the opening even more, he could peer in and see the pages. They appeared to be whole, not fragmented, but still he used all his skills in dealing with old documents to make certain that when he pulled them out, they would not tear. They were degrading over the entire surface, and he could tell they were becoming brittle.

He successfully extracted the three pages without damaging them and separated them in front of him. They were written in uncials in Koine Greek, the same dialect as on the outside strap of the larger pouch. Except for a few words near the end of the entire document, the letters were small and compact, making use of all the parchment. At his reading of the first few words, Basil's breath caught in his throat. The document began:

**ΠΑΥΛΟϹΑΠΟϹΤΟΛΟϹΔΙΑΘЄΛΗΜΑΤΟϹΘЄΟΥ
ΧΡΙϹΤΟΥΙΗϹΟΥΤΟΙϹ ΟΥϹΙΝ ЄΝΛΑΟΔΙΚЄΙΑ**
(Paul an apostle of Jesus Christ by the will of God to the saints in Laodicea)

Basil began reading the letter with wide-eyed incredulity, not quite believing what he had before him. On the one hand, he knew of a Latin "letter to Laodicea" included in the Vulgate as early as the 4th century; the Western Church's Pope Gregory spoke of it, and by the 6th century there was a version that accompanied the Vulgate, though it was not considered canonical. But no one knew of a Greek letter to Laodicea, and the Latin one had been condemned as a forgery since the time of Jerome, about the time it appeared. Yet here was a Greek manuscript purporting to be from Paul to Laodicea, and Basil knew it was quite, quite old. In fact, at first reading he realized it wasn't at all like the Latin version, which was very short. This letter was several pages long. Was there any way it could be the original letter from Paul's hand?

Basil pored over the text for an hour or more, noting where Paul—or whoever wrote it—had included thoughts similar to his letters to the Colossian and Philippian churches, but not the same wording. He paid particular note to the personal reference to someone named Akakios. Looking quickly at the notes that had been outside the pouch, he saw they had been penned by someone named Illyus at the Church of Antioch, and they went to some length to describe Akakios, identifying him as the person who entrusted the sealed pouch to Illyus, holding him to an oath not to open it, and not telling him what was in it. Illyus had apparently agreed to store or secure the documents, not even knowing they were documents, but believing that the contents had something to do with Akakios and the church at Laodicea.

What the author of this letter said about Akakios pretty much told the story of why he had traveled to Antioch. He had intercepted the letter meant for the church, because the letter indicted Akakios for heretical beliefs. Apparently, Akakios was possessed of just enough fearful respect for a writing by Paul that he couldn't bring himself to simply destroy the letter, but only to conceal it, perhaps meaning to deal with it in some other way later. Was he going to copy the letter, attempting to reproduce Paul's hand? That way, Akakios could have left out the reference to himself. Perhaps that's what he intended to do, but never did.

Basil sat back in his chair and remained motionless for nearly an hour, pondering, wondering, worrying, thinking. He was the curator now of what he had to believe was what it said it was, and like Illyus a thousand years before him, he didn't know what to do with it other than keep it secure and private for the present. The subjects and contents of the letter would not rock the Christian world to its core—they didn't contradict or even add to the substance of the teaching of Christ or the Apostles, in Basil's view—but the mere existence of this letter, if it were believed by the Eastern or Western churches to be genuine, would certainly cause a stir. It might even be added to the issues over which Eastern and Western churches were presently divided, hastening their split. A formal schism was inevitable, Basil thought, and probably soon, but why add fuel to the fire?

A trip to Constantinople

Late in the year 1049, Basil put the manuscript into a new leather pouch, and he planned a trip to see his counterpart in the library of the great Church of Constantinople, a certain Ioannes Ponti. Ioannes had been a confidant of his some years in the past. Perhaps he would have some wisdom to impart in the matter.

In 1051, Basil gained leave of his bishop to travel to Constantinople, on a visit he described as professional in nature. He was still heavily engaged in the thorough cataloguing of the Syriac church's library, and Ioannes had, according to reports, completed such a reorganization of Constantinople's much larger collection. Basil took with him the pouch containing the letter, prepared to show it to Ioannes if he felt the time were right.

Arriving in Constantinople, he spent several days with Ioannes, studying his methods and looking at some of the documents of great value. At one point, he broached the subject of the hypothetical existence of a genuine letter of Paul to Laodicea.

Ioannes, who did not suspect (as Basil wrote later) that Basil actually had such a letter, opined that if such a document were to exist and were proven—at least reasonably—to be genuine, it would be invaluable. But, as they agreed, the letter Marcion claimed to have seen or possessed was no doubt a forgery if it even had existed. And where, after all, could the genuine letter have been all this time?

Hypothetically, however, Ioannes said that if he came into possession of a letter claimed to be genuine, he would probably keep the matter secret until it could be exhaustively studied as to its contents, its age, and its provenance. In no event would he publicize it immediately, especially if anything in it even hinted at new doctrine or even a shade of an interpretation of existing doctrine that was unheard of. Basil changed the subject shortly, and they spent another day going through Constantinople's library. Basil informed Ioannes he would be leaving at first light, and they said their goodbyes.

That evening, Basil made a momentous decision. In the chamber provided him for his brief stay, he sat down and wrote a few pages of notes to include in the pouch that already contained the manuscript of the letter to Laodicea and the notes written presumably a thousand years ago by Illyus of Antioch. In his own notes, Basil recounted how he had discovered the documents and where they had been in all probability for a great length of time, and he explained his replacement of the original leather container. He also gave some brief opinions as to what he, as a librarian, thought of the relative importance of both the letter and the notes signed by Illyus. In a separate, personal note addressed to Ioannes, he apologized for leaving the packet without giving it to him personally, but he defended his doing so by reminding him of their conversation two days before, saying he was confident that Ioannes would deal with the documents wisely. He re-wrapped the new pouch and went to bed. Early in the morning he went into Ioannes's workroom and left the pouch on his desk for him to discover. Then he left quickly for home.

Ioannes Ponti opened the pouch on his desk when he began his work for the day, reading first the personal note from Basil and then looking at the underlying documents. His first reading of the purported letter from Paul to Laodicea was with professional skepticism, but like Basil, after a few days of rereading and reflection, he was eventually overwhelmed with the importance of the document, believing it to be genuine in all probability.

He also remembered rendering the opinion that it would be injudicious to publicize such a document. And he didn't.

Instead, he wrote an account of his meeting with Basil, included a few notes about the contents of the letter itself, and re-sealed everything in the new leather pouch Basil had brought. His plan was to think the matter through thoroughly, pray about what should be done with the letter, and take action in a few months.

A few months turned into a year, and Ioannes's initial excitement waned as doubts crept in. While he had never had plans for wholesale publication of the letter, now he pondered what would be the response of his own bishop and others who might have some power over his future in the church. With increasing distance of time since his acquisition of the documents, Ioannes was able to dismiss any thought of them from his mind, even occasionally revising his previous opinion that they were genuine in the first place. He decided to store the sealed pouch in the Constantinople library, identifying it on the outside as private correspondence attributed to some person with a name no one would recognize, and appearing to be a volume of no interest to anyone. He placed the volume in the recesses of the library where he would know about it, but no one else would come across it easily and become curious.

Early in the Year of Our Lord 1052, two years before the Great Schism in the Church, Ioannes suffered a heart attack and died quite unexpectedly. The now disguised and visually unimportant leather pouch occupied its niche in the deep recesses of the Constantinople church library through the curatorship of another, and another, and yet another librarian. It was moved now and then as buildings were built and renovated, but like so many volumes that are stored, moved, dusted, stored again, glanced at and then forgotten, it was both seen and invisible, not to be opened and discovered for another

450 years.

12 • DESIDERIUS ERASMUS

MARKOS LOUKIOS, who had grown up mostly in Athens, Greece, moved with his family to Constantinople in the waning years of the A.D. 1400s. He was accepted into the priesthood in 1499, and became a companion curator of the library at the Constantinople Church. Upon the death of his co-curator, Petronas in 1515, Markos assumed all the responsibilities of librarian, and undertook a thorough review of what the library contained. No one had done so for at least a century, he believed, and there were many ancient volumes that needed to be inspected and their preservation ensured.

It was in 1516, in the course of Markos's putting eyes and hands on every volume in the substantial collection, that he saw a packet of personal correspondence attributed to an obscure name, and opened it to see if it contained anything that should be kept at all. What he found interrupted the process of re-cataloguing the library for a solid week.

Markos was at first incredulous, stunned. Then he became

excited, but still highly skeptical. After a day or so he began engaging in audible debate with himself, muttering in the privacy of his chambers and carrying on a vigorous argument that one of him seemed to be winning. Finally, he progressed to conviction. This was the find of a lifetime. The find of many lifetimes.

The Letter of Paul the Apostle to the Church at Laodicea was remarkable in itself, of course. It addressed a theological troublemaker in the person of one Akakios; it exalted the Lordship of Jesus Christ both in heaven and earth; it stated core doctrines of the Christian faith in ways similar to but varied from other general epistles; and it emphasized the urgency of the church's witness in the world through both life and word. The documents that were included in the packet with the Letter itself, however, were astounding. They revealed that at least three persons had known of the existence of the letter: Akakios, who had purloined it the year it was written, probably A.D. 61; Basil, a librarian at Antioch who had opened it in 1049; and Ioannes, a librarian in Constantinople who received it from Basil in 1051. In addition, a fourth person, the librarian to whom Akakios had given the sealed letter, a certain Illyus of Antioch, had not known for certain the contents of the sealed packet but had been suspicious of Akakios's motive and had guessed they were documents that would embarrass him somehow.

Markos concluded that what he held was genuine, in part

because its previous curators had been fearful and cautious about ever revealing what they had. That alone suggested powerfully that after their study of the documents, they had been convinced the letter from Paul was what it said it was, and they wanted to protect the church at large from the controversy that might ensue if they went public.

Markos was more intrepid than his forebears. He had always thought of himself as being brave, and for good or ill he was little concerned with what others thought of him. And he had always hoped he would be able to do something important in his lifetime, something for which generations to come would remember him. In his mind, this didn't make him guilty of great hubris, only the desire that his life would influence the lives of others, beyond even the way that a priest affected the spiritual well being of the Christians in his care.

When he lived in Greece, Markos had frequently seen his cousins from Rome, the children of his mother's sister who had married a prominent churchman there. The cousins, three in his family and four in his aunt's, were inter-spaced in ages and had visited each other's homes every two years or so, when they could afford the cost and time to make the trip of some 700 miles, including passage on a ship. Markos had loved seeing Rome, and while he was the son of a faithful Orthodox churchman, and in no danger of switching from East to West, he thought the traditions and the churches were closer than each side insisted they were. Even as he sought the priesthood in his own tradition, he had cultivated friendships across the great divide, and he kept up with the goings-on in the Roman Catholic Church.

Across the great divide

Like everyone in the Christian world, Markos followed the developing rift in the Roman fellowship that seemed destined to break into open conflict. And he became aware of an emerging theological leader by the name of Desiderius Erasmus, a Netherlands-born cleric and scholar who had begun to make a name for himself through teaching at Oxford, England, in 1499, the same year Markos became a priest in the Orthodox Church. By 1515 when Markos took full responsibility for the Constantinople library, Erasmus was working on his first printing of a Greek-Latin New Testament. Markos obtained a copy of it through his sources in a network extending through Greece, Hungary, Bohemia, and to the North Sea. He was always obtaining new books, as well as news by way of letters and a few printed sheets circulating between libraries and other institutions.

Of Erasmus there was not an equal in the Greek churches, at least in the opinion of Markos Loukios. Within hours of his discovery of the lost Letter to the Church at Laodicea, Markos decided that Erasmus, scholar of Greek and Latin, should see it. Markos was quite familiar, of course, with the history of forgeries of this letter, and of the fact that there was a Latin version purporting to have been a translation of the Greek original, but which was dismissed as a 4th-century forgery by the Roman Church even as they kept re-copying it to include along with versions of the Vulgate. This didn't make any sense to Markos, but a number of things the Roman Church did weren't entirely sensible in his opinion. But here—here was the original letter, no doubt. It wasn't a Greek version of the earlier, spurious Latin letter, but an entirely different letter, longer, and in Koine Greek uncials. Surely if Erasmus had it, the Letter of Paul to the Church at Laodicea would finally be known to the world and attested as genuine.

In 1518, Markos would be up for a sabbatical, and he could take the letter to Erasmus himself. But he didn't wish to wait for three years to find Erasmus and put the letter in his hands. And after all, he had not had any sort of introduction to Erasmus, though he believed he could manage to secure a reference through ecclesiastical friends in Europe. Still, time seemed to be of the essence. Erasmus was about fifty years old, and there was no guarantee that he—or Markos for that matter, who was only a year younger—would be around for many years to come. He decided to strike while the iron was hot.

Markos decided to use his own funds, which due to his father's wealth were considerable, to contract with a courier to take a package and correspondence to Erasmus, who at the time was living in Leuven, Belgium, and teaching at the University there. In his letters he introduced himself, named a few acquaintances whom he believed they had in common, and explained his urgent interest in Erasmus's study of the document purporting to be the Laodicean letter.

Markos realized he would be surrendering the original letter to the possible vagaries of fate—not that he believed in fate—risking its safety through travel over a long distance. It went without saying that he was going to copy the letter: whether it was genuine or not, the text had to be preserved. He suffered a spell of possessiveness over the original manuscript, of which it seemed obvious no copies existed, until he made one shortly. But if he wanted a linguistic expert and scholar of first rank to see and study it, he would have to risk its security for the exigency of that hour in history. And after all, a professional courier service was usually quite secure, if one spent the money to hire the best; and he did.

In late 1515, the courier he employed left Constantinople for parts east and north, some 1,400 miles as crows fly, though no crows flew that far. It would take a few weeks for the courier to make his way to the University of Leuven. He bore the pouch containing the letter and its attendant documents, and the message from Markos, which also requested that when Erasmus had made full use of the documents, he would return them, at Markos's expense, to Constantinople. The courier had instructions to return with any written response that Erasmus might want to send, including—though Markos hoped not—the return of the letter itself, if Erasmus should reject accepting the missive outright.

Several weeks elapsed after the courier departed with the precious packet. Markos Loukios, not normally given to nervousness, became steadily more anxious about the courier's success and expectant for his reappearance on the doorstep. He reassured himself of the reliability of quality courier services these days, and while he ate too much some days and too little on others while dealing with his preoccupation with the yet-to-be-completed mission, otherwise he suffered only the jitters of distraction.

When the courier returned at long last, he gave a short note to Markos, in which Erasmus promised to study the documents carefully and return them, as Markos had promised repayment. Now that the letter was in Erasmus's hands, Markos waited patiently for whatever would happen next.

In 1516, one of the twenty-year reappearances of the Black Death swept through Constantinople, and unfortunately for Markos Loukios, he became one of its first victims. Among his effects dealt with upon his death were notifications to be sent far and wide to his many family members and a few clerics across the great East-West divide, and a sealed letter for Erasmus in Belgium, a letter Markos had fortuitously prepared shortly after hearing back from Erasmus. Upon receiving and opening the letter, Erasmus read:

I write this letter to be sent to you upon my death,

should I not have heard from you concerning the manuscript I sent by courier. This is to inform you that I do hereby bequeath to you the materials I sent, for you to do with as you please and think best. —Markos Loukios, Librarian of the Church of Constantinople."

Markos also left instructions for his family to destroy a sealed packet of personal papers by burning them. Included was his three-page copy of the Letter to Laodicea, which he had produced before sending the original to Erasmus.

Late that same year in 1516, Erasmus published his *Novum Instrumentum omne,* a Greek New Testament. In 1519, he published a second edition, renaming it the *Novum Testamentum,* which Luther employed in his German translation. In 1522, Erasmus published yet a third edition, which William Tyndale used for his English translation in 1526, and which ultimately became part of the *Textus Receptus,* the basis for the King James Version translators.

During all this time, Erasmus continued to study and labor over the Markos Loukios Manuscript, as he referred to it in a note that he eventually included with the documents. He decided it was wise not to act hastily in the matter, and it was shelved securely for weeks at a time while he pondered now and again what he would do.

Since Markos hadn't lived to see the return of the pouch and its documents, he was unable to add any postscript upon their return from Erasmus. However, Erasmus saw the pattern of transmission notes from caretaker to caretaker of the manuscript of the Laodicean letter, and now as one of the caretakers himself, he included notes of his own to document what was taking place with this historical artifact. He added a running description of what he did with the letter during momentous hours in church history.

Erasmus was busy with his teaching and translating in 1516 and 1517, and then he moved somewhat abruptly in 1517 to Basel, Switzerland, continuing his studies and other writing there. He finally determined that he would entrust the Laodicean letter to another scholar. He had decided not to publish the letter anyway, and so he was not giving up the notoriety that might attend being the one to reveal the existence of the letter to the Christian world.

On the prospect of his parting with the letter, he wrote that he had completed a thorough study of the manuscript and could find nothing to contradict its genuineness. He noted that the parchment was becoming quite fragile, and that in spite of the reinforcement of the leather pouch intended to keep the document flat and protected, the manuscript was cracked in several places and in danger of falling apart. He documented his making a copy of it on current paper with the best of inks.

Erasmus also translated the Greek manuscript into Latin—a curious decision from the perspective of the 21st century, but thoroughly understandable from his own perspective. Erasmus was a devoted Roman Catholic, and the language of the Church, kept alive by the constant use of priests throughout Europe and beyond, was Latin. A Latin version of the Laodicean letter would be more useful than the Greek to the rank and file priests who weren't scholars of either Greek or Hebrew. However, Erasmus wrote of his deep hesitation to make public the existence of the letter, and his Greek copy and Latin translation simply went into the pouch, which he sealed until he could do with it what he had in mind.

What he had in mind near the end of 1517 might have seemed out of character for him, especially considering his devotion to the Church of Rome. The growing tension within the church over calls for reformation had produced, through the fires of controversy, emerging leaders of change, including most notably Martin Luther. Just a month or so before, news spread like wildfire that Luther had distributed widely throughout Germany a document he titled *Ninety-Five Theses,* challenging the teachings and actions of the Church and the Pope. There were reports he had nailed a copy of the one-sheet document to the door of the Church at Wittenberg. Upon seeing a copy of the *Theses* in December, Erasmus was at once appalled and intrigued.

Though Erasmus contended with Martin Luther over certain issues in the growing movement for reformation, he had conflicting views within himself about what would or should happen in the matter of the scriptures. He was very much aware that his printed versions of the Greek New Testament would be used to make English and possibly other translations. He didn't disagree with the principle of translating the scriptures, quite obviously, because the Greek had long been set aside in favor of the Church's use of the Latin Vulgate. Whether it were appropriate for the Bible to be translated into yet other languages was the issue. He did not himself translate the scriptures into even his own native language, preferring to read them in the official language of the Roman Church. Nevertheless, he prepared a polished version of the Greek New Testament that he knew instinctively would be used eventually to put the scriptures into the languages of the people. He could see the handwriting, as it were, on the wall.

Sometime in 1518, Erasmus returned to their pouch: the original manuscript of the Laodicean letter; the copy he had made of the letter in Greek; the Latin translation of the letter he had done; the notes written by Illyus as copied by Basil; the notes Basil had added to the growing stack; the notes written by Ioannes of Constantinople; the notes composed by Markos Loukios, also of Constantinople; his own notes, detailing his creation of the Greek copy and Latin translation; and a separate note showing his assessment of the letter as absolutely genuine. He sealed the pouch and prepared it for transmission by special courier to London.

The courier arrived in London late in 1518 and delivered the package and its introductory correspondence to John Colet, a prebendary of St. Paul's Cathedral. Erasmus became friends with Colet in 1499 when he went to England and taught at the University of Oxford, where Colet had been lecturing for three years. Influenced in part by his familiarity with the fiery preaching of Florence's Giolama Savonarola, Colet had reformist views that were bolder than those Erasmus had allowed himself to possess so far. Consequently, Colet was sometimes accused of believing and teaching heresy. This charge self-evidently came out of the fact that he persistently and roundly condemned the avarice, immorality, lustfulness, hedonism, excess, worldliness and covetousness of priests. His scathing rebukes obviously struck home, and his targets returned fire with the dreaded epithet of heresy. Privately, Erasmus applauded his friend and former mentor.

Colet and Erasmus stood on the cusp of the Protestant Reformation, wanting to reform their own church without separating from it, but sensing that reform would give way to revolution and give birth to something altogether different. It was this common spirit shared by the two that made Colet the one person Erasmus decided should determine what to do with the Letter of Paul the Apostle to the Church at Laodicea. Perhaps Erasmus simply hesitated to be the one to go public with what would be a controversial document, though he had gladly taken controversial stances before. But he truly believed Colet would be the better man to uncover the secret letter.

13 • JOHN COLET

ON THE AFTERNOON a courier arrived at St. Paul's in London bearing a package for Dean John Colet, he was directed to Colet's chambers and there presented an aging leather pouch, affixed with the seal of Erasmus. Colet spoke with the courier briefly, who didn't know what the pouch contained and couldn't offer much in the way of personal knowledge of how Erasmus fared, his not being a close friend of the European scholar. Colet dismissed him with great gratitude after offering him something to eat, which the courier politely declined.

Colet sat down with the package and broke the seal. Withdrawing the documents inside, he first read the message from his friend Erasmus. Startled by what it said, he then slowly and carefully read each page in the aging stack, finally gazing at both the Latin and Greek documents on which were written the words attributed to the Apostle Paul, to the Church at Laodicea. When he finished, he read the Greek document again, and yet again. Then he sat for nearly an hour, warmed by the sunlight coming in through his chamber window, chilled by the immense significance of the letter, should it prove, as Erasmus had already concluded it did, to be genuine.

Finally he replaced the documents in the pouch, secured it among his other books, and almost as if he feared it would disappear if he left it, he went to the door, gazing back at it several times, and went to the chapel, where he prostrated himself in prayer for a long while, until the light streaming in through multicolored panes high above him dimmed and began to leave him in darkness. Then he left, not hungry as he would have been under normal circumstances, and he returned to his chamber where he lighted several candles, retrieved the packet, and read through all its contents yet again, further absorbing their impact.

Colet rearranged his time around his lectures in the next two weeks and spent every moment he could doing research, availing himself of the considerable library of St. Paul's. Precious little had been written about the Laodicean letter referred to in Colossians. Colet was familiar with a Latin document claimed by some to be that letter, which sometimes accompanied the Vulgate New Testament. It was Colet's understanding that few congregations in the Eastern Church thought this purported letter of Paul to Laodicea was genuine, but quite a few parishioners in the Western Church did think the Latin document was Pauline. However, nothing much was made of it, since the canon did not include it. At the Council of Florence held in 1439-1443 a few years before Colet was born, the See of Rome had categorically declared there are fourteen Pauline epistles, and they did not include the Laodicean Letter. Colet knew that no current scholar worthy of the name thought the Latin letter was original to the Apostle, but the subject was not high on anyone's list of important topics of debate.

The Latin letter

Colet located the text of the currently known letter. Its Latin text was available with the Vulgate, and Colet had a copy somewhere in his personal library. The infamous Martin Luther had translated it into German, and Colet had tried to come by a copy of that translation but had been so far unsuccessful. He did, however, have a copy of the Middle English translation done by Wycliffe's followers about 1394, after Wycliffe's death. He retrieved this and the Latin text from a dusty corner of his shelves and sat down to re-familiarized himself with the no-doubt fraudulent letter.

Its nineteen verses were terse and choppy. If there had been a Greek manuscript behind it—and Colet was quite certain there never had been—it would have been an unusually poor, disjointed writing to have come from Paul's pen :

1 Paul, an apostle not of men nor by man, but by Jesus

Christ, to the brethren that are at Laodicea.
2 Grace be to you and peace from God the Father and our Lord Jesus Christ.
3 I thank Christ in every prayer of mine, that you may continue and persevere in good works, looking for that which is promised in the day of judgment.
4 Do not be troubled by the vain speeches of anyone who perverts the truth, that they may draw you aside from the truth of the gospel which I have preached.
5 And now may God grant that my converts may attain to a perfect knowledge of the truth of the gospel, be beneficent, and doing good works which accompany salvation.
6 And now my bonds, which I suffer in Christ, are manifest, in which I rejoice and am glad.
7 For I know that this shall turn to my salvation forever, which shall be through your prayer and the supply of the Holy Spirit.
8 Whether I live or die, to me to live shall be a life to Christ; to die will be joy.
9 And our Lord will grant us his mercy, that you may have the same love and be like-minded.
10 Wherefore, my beloved, as you have heard of the coming of the Lord, so think and act reverently, and it shall be to you life eternal;
11 For it is God who is working in you;
12 And do all things without sin.
13 And what is best, my beloved: rejoice in the Lord Jesus Christ, and avoid all filthy lucre.
14 Let all your requests by made known to God, and be steady in the doctrine of Christ.

15 And whatever things are sound and true, and of good
report, and chaste, and just, and lovely, these things do.
16 Those things which you have heard and received,
think on these things, and peace shall be with you.
17 All the saints salute you.
18 The grace of our Lord Jesus Christ be with your spirit.
Amen.
19 Cause this Epistle to be read to the Colossians, and the
Epistle of the Colossians to be read among you.

Comparing the choppy, awkward text of the Latin claimant to the Laodicean letter to the much more fluid and cogent text of what he had received from Erasmus, Colet thought to himself that here was yet another indication of the authenticity of the document. The short Latin document read almost like a child's invention; the longer Greek document he had before him practically begged to be ascribed to Paul himself.

Finally famished, Colet sought out a flat loaf of bread he kept in his rooms, and he munched on it while he pondered the future of his remarkable packet of documents. First, of course, he would send a letter back to Erasmus, thanking him for the manuscripts. While he was thinking about it, he went to his writing desk, withdrew paper, and wrote the letter. Then he sat and thought about his options.

Instinctively, he thought this was something he should share with at least one other, perhaps a scholar, but perhaps only a superior, whether he were a scholar or not. In fact, he began to believe it would be best not to involve another scholar; to do so would invite contradiction. To inform a superior would be appropriate, and if it were someone who was unlikely to want to be engaged in a co-study of the letter, it would leave Colet alone to evaluate the letter from a scholarly standpoint.

It became obvious before long that his best course was to inform the Archbishop himself of what he had.

William Warham had been Archbishop of Canterbury for the past fourteen years. He and John Colet were relatively close friends, though something like flint on steel now and then. Colet was more of a reformer than Warham, who himself held views that at times made him seem amenable to reform but who then abruptly showed his other side rather than make waves. The occasional call for Colet to be prosecuted by the Church for some heresy was ignored or dismissed summarily by Warham, who took his cue from King Henry's great esteem for Colet.

Warham was also a busy man. In addition to being the Archbishop of Canterbury—enough responsibility in itself—he was also the Chancellor of Oxford University. Between his duties regarding these two positions and his more than occasional audiences with the King, he was probably incapable of, and would probably be uninterested in, involving himself in the study of an arcane manuscript that Colet would not energetically attempt to convince him was genuine. Colet could dutifully inform a superior of something that might affect the church, not just himself; but he could be reasonably assured that the Archbishop would not interfere with his private study and evaluation of the Laodicean letter.

In the deepening night as his candles burned low, Colet decided to go to the Archbishop before week's end, bearing the leather packet of documents.

With the morning's light his feelings had changed. Probably he would inform Archbishop Warham eventually, but for the present, he would take the Laodicean letter and its attendant documents to the library at the Archbishop's palace, where it would be more safely stored, and where he might have exclusive access to it among the archives. He would then make a visit every two weeks or so and spend some hours availing himself of the voluminous Lambath Palace Library, the central library for the Church throughout England. The Lambath Palace was the residence of the Archbishop, whoever that might be, and it also housed the Archbishopric's extensive library, which had been amassing its impressive collection since the early 1200s. Colet could formally request of the Archbishop that the librarian secure his volume in an archive, with Colet as the solely authorized person to view it.

Colet first prepared a new and more protected enclosure for the documents. He sketched out a design and took it to a local leather craftsman. The design called for a thick portfolio, thirty five inches wide, intended to be folded in thirds. The inside, right third had a pocket capable of comfortably enclosing the documents, and it was fortified with a sheet of brass underneath the outside surface. The entire portfolio was lined with silk. The pocketed side would fold toward the center, the left side would fold over the right, and the folded unit would be about ten inches wide and thirteen inches tall. Straps at top and bottom would secure the portfolio and would have small locks on them. The left edge would have a brass plate engraved with the words, "John Colet: Correspondence."

There was no deception in the description of the packet as containing correspondence, quite obviously. There were letters of all the previous caretakers of the Laodicean letter, and of course, the letter itself was the correspondence of Paul. The Lambath Library's curator would be under instructions to allow access to Colet alone, and in any event Colet would have the only key to the locks.

When the leather craftsman sent word to Colet that the portfolio was finished, Colet picked it up and paid him handsomely, even more than he had contracted for. He put the letter and other documents in the new portfolio and sent word to the Archbishop that he should like to visit with him briefly the following week. The Archbishop sent word that it would be a few weeks before he could accommodate his friend, and that he would send for him when he could.

Visiting the Archbishop

The year turned to 1519 before Colet received an invitation

to visit Archbishop Warham. It was a cold, late January day when Warham had Colet ushered in. After formal greetings as befitted the two churchmen, Warham dismissed attendants and the two were alone.

Colet held up the portfolio briefly without calling special attention to it, but said that he had brought it with the hope of having it entered, for a brief time anyway, into the Lambath Library where it would be secure and he could access it at his leisure. He laid the portfolio aside in a casual manner that suggested he would move the conversation along to more important things. Warham didn't probe the matter any further, other than to say he would issue an instruction to Charles Henry, then the library's curator, to admit the volume to a controlled archive with John Colet as the solely authorized viewer of it. Done.

Colet launched into several other topics he had contrived to fill their remaining time, which was not more than a quarter of an hour, and then he begged leave of the Archbishop in order that he might not take up any more of Warham's no doubt busy day. Before Colet left, Warham summoned an aide and scribbled a note to him for Charles Henry, with which the aide left immediately. Then Warham and Colet said goodbye.

Colet made his way through the palace to the Lambath Library, where Charles Henry, an amicable but distracted looking man, met him and showed him to a cubicle deep in the back of the library, telling him his volume would be kept there, and the door would be locked to all but authorized persons, who could access the cubicle only one at a time.

Colet thanked him and returned to St. Paul's. Charles Henry returned to his duties, meaning to follow through with recording the John Colet volume, trusting the note scribbled by Warham to remind him, but inadvertently discarding that note with a pile of papers headed for the dustbin.

Interrupted study

The year 1519 was a busy one for the always busy John Colet, consumed with preaching, teaching, study and exegesis, administration, and officious duties engaging with other church leaders around London and elsewhere. He planned to go to the Lambath Library in two weeks, but became busier still and didn't go. It got to be late summer, and he still hadn't gone to study the volume. In fact, he was keeping to himself for the most part, due to a wave of the sweating sickness coursing across England since early August. Outbreaks had taken place in England every few years since 1485. Fearing he would contract the mysterious and quickly deadly disease, he stayed in his chambers except for official duties.

On the sixteenth of that month, however, he was overcome with chills, which lasted three hours and then turned suddenly to profuse sweating, which exhausted him and sent him into delirium. An aide looked in on him midday and found him asleep. An hour later, he was still asleep, but now no more to wake.

In addition to his not finishing his studies of the Laodicean packet and letter, he had also not amended his will to include what should be done with the volume he had arranged to be secured at the Lambath Library. Charles Henry, the curator, had been replaced by another curator in mid summer of that year, and the new curator had no idea he had a private volume in his library belonging to the recently departed John Colet, and no record of it, either. The Library continued to enjoy the curatorship of a succession of capable men for another three hundred seventy-five years before the fine leather portfolio deep in one of its private cubicles was disturbed.

An ancient find

Outside the dark and quiet cubicle, outside the palace walls, and across the whole of England, what came to be known as the Protestant Reformation smouldered, burned, and raged. At the Diet of Speyer in 1526, the Catholic Church branded the movement against Roman authority as Protestantism, and the condemnation was embraced by those who sought the kind of reform that would actually separate them from the Church of Rome. England's King Henry VIII sought an annulment from his wife Catherine, who in eighteen years of marriage had not produced a son. By that time, Henry had also banished Catherine from court and given her rooms to Anne Boleyn. Pope Clement refused to annul Henry's marriage, and a succession of interwoven events, most of them more political than theological, led Henry to reject the authority of the Pope. With the cooperation of Parliament, he initiated the separation of the Church in England from the Roman Church in 1534.

Life at the Lambath Library continued unabated. Erasmus died in 1536 not knowing that the Letter to the Church at Laodicea had been stored by his friend John Colet in England's premiere library or that Colet had not made any arrangements for the letter's future other than to allow it to sit at the back of a dark shelf for more than three centuries.

Many years later, England planted colonies in a new world, which then protested her oppressive domination. The protestors of the Protestants in England sought a place to worship their own way, not under the pope-like monarch of Britain. The colonists also sought political independence and gained it through war. Finally accepting the facts of history, England eventually became the firmest of friends with the United States, and planted some of its churches on America's shores. The Episcopal Church, part of the worldwide Anglican Communion, came to share with the Church of England just about everything but the requirement that its clergy swear allegiance to its king or queen. Collegial relationships abounded between clergy on either side of the Atlantic pond, adding to the fundamentally kindred spirit between former Empire and colony, and helping to create the most fast friendship of any two nations on earth.

14 • William Adams

In England in 1995, the talk around the Lambath Palace and Library was that in a few years a new building would house its more than 120,000 books and archives that had belonged to its succession of Archbishops of Canterbury. It would eventually be more than twenty years before the plans took shape, but meanwhile, assistant curators and their assistant underlings scurried around the Palace Library updating the catalogue, dusting long-untouched volumes, and generally performing spring cleaning. One of these assistants was assigned to the archive where the ancient, fine leather volume of John Colet's letters rested, behind other large volumes virtually untouched for generations. In the course of his work, the assistant handled the leather portfolio, but without opening it since it was locked.

In order to keep the assistant's identity secret, I will refer to him/her as a male, and assign the name James Marston. James wondered if his priest would be interested in seeing the volume bearing John Colet's name. His priest had recently waxed eloquent from the pulpit about the courage of reformers hundreds of years before, and had called the name of John Colet. The assistant had hitherto been only vaguely familiar with this particular figure from the days surrounding the Protestant Reformation in England. While he didn't open the volume, its tarnished but quite legible plate on the spine of the locked portfolio clearly said it was correspondence belonging to John Colet.

On a Sunday in June, rainy as usual, assistant Marston approached the Rev'd William Adams (who, like the assistant, kept his identity private in the matter; I have randomly chosen the name "Adams" to refer to him here) and told him what he had found in the Lambath Library. It turned out that Adams didn't exactly have a special interest in Colet, but he was casually interested in history, and he agreed to come see the assistant at the library in a week or so, since the assistant could not take the volume out of the library, but he believed he would be able to authorize the Rev'd William Adams to see it.

During the following week Marston searched the paper and card files of the library that had not yet been entered into digital format, for a record pertaining to "John Colet: Correspondence." He couldn't find anything. The leather enclosure of the volume and the style of lettering engraved on the brass plate, strongly suggested it originated in Colet's time, but it was possible it was later. However, the lack of a record was curious. Ordinarily, archival volumes would have records indicating conditions of their being kept, authority of access, and the like.

In the absence of such a record, the assistant felt warranted to grant access to Adams to see the volume, and when Adams visited the second week after being informed of this item of interest, Marston showed him the cubicle and presented him with the leather bound portfolio.

They both noted that the portfolio was secured by two straps with locks. The assistant apologetically said he had been unable to locate any record of the portfolio and that he presumed the key to the locks would have belonged either to Colet or to whomever entered the portfolio into the library to begin with. Adams said he was quite delighted simply to see the volume on this occasion, and that he would probably return with a friend who was a leather expert and might be able to inspect the volume and give him an opinion as to its age.

Adams admitted later in a roundabout way that his intention was to bring a friend who was a locksmith who would be able to get into the portfolio in seconds. Adams was both shameful and defensive about this action, on the basis of what he found when he eventually got into the portfolio. By then, the ends had justified the means.

When Adams returned with a "Mr Smith," James Marston left them alone momentarily and Smith picked the ancient locks with little difficulty. Smith then excused himself. Moldy documents didn't interest him.

Adams extracted the papers, read them all with increasing excitement, having a bit of trouble with the Latin and much more with the Greek. He had eked out passing marks in Greek, decades ago, and had lost most of his vocabulary. But he remembered the alphabet, which was like the English alphabet here and there, and it wasn't hard for him to make out and translate the first words of the oldest parchment:

> Paul, an apostle of the Lord Jesus Christ by the will of God, to the Saints which are at Laodicea…

Even without being able to decipher some of the older writings, Adams knew he was looking at something extraordinary. And it was something he coveted for himself. In a half hour's time he had hatched a plan to gain possession of this portfolio. He thanked the assistant on his way out, telling him that he had replaced the volume on the back of the shelf where it had stayed. He had, in fact, done so, but before he did, he used a pocket knife to bend a hooked part of the lock on each of the straps so that it could be inserted in the half affixed to the body of the portfolio, but would not engage. The lock would not lock.

The Rev'd William Adams returned the following day saying he wished to photograph the portfolio, and he had brought a camera with him. He had also worn his mac, since it was raining modestly that day, and he carried a brolly. Doffing the macintosh inside, he got down to business in the cubicle photographing the portfolio. The assistant, Marston, had done his part in the whole matter, having no personal interest in the correspondence of John Colet, and he assumed Adams would return the volume to the shelves when he finished. Adams indicated he would, hinted that he was not likely to return—too many other duties to attend to—and he was presently alone.

In ten minutes, the portfolio folded neatly under his mac, the Rev'd William Adams exited the cubicle, shut its gate, strode quietly through the library to the door, extended his brolly against the light drizzle, and left, not to return at all.

Adams was no scholar, none at all. His remarks about John Colet from the pulpit recently were gleaned from a history book in his small personal library. He could re-type book materials with the best of them and make himself sound erudite and well read. He had gone far with this approach. But now in possession of one of the more surprising finds of all time—if it were genuine—Adams didn't exactly know what course to take.

He didn't know how to evaluate the manuscript for its authenticity. He wasn't familiar enough with the manuscripts of other, possibly related documents, or the repositories where they might be found, to know where to go, whom to see, what to read, what to study. He was really a hack, and in his honest hours, which were few but did exist, he admitted it to himself.

He was competent enough for his local duties, but not more, and it didn't take him long to realize that there was no real future in his attempting to study the purported Letter to Laodicea for himself and make any kind of report to the scholarly world. They might, and probably would, laugh him off the stage.

He did, however, have some instincts about the value of mysterious items to other people, such as collectors. Someone out there would pay a pretty penny for the documents he had.

Throughout the remainder of 1995 the Rev'd W. Adams made several surreptitious contacts with vaguely worded suggestions that planted the idea that a certain rector might, just might, have some documents of great antiquity that would be of great value and could be had for valuable consideration. He was apparently fishing in a dead pond, however, and no one bit.

An occasional, new idea struck him during 1996 and he tried several other ways to contact the black market without revealing his own identity, but with no success. He considered going completely above board and speaking to one of the other bishops, but where was the excitement in that? Or the profit? Above the board there was certainly no money to be had, and someone else would get the attention that would come to the person who did the scholarly work. In fact, if he told another priest, he could count on the bishop's finding out, and when that happened, the secret would be no more. For the moment, he sat on what he had.

In fact, as the year dragged on, he became less and less excited about the old portfolio and less inclined to believe that it was genuine. Doubts crept in. Why was it in the library? Why hadn't a previous possessor of it gone public? Would any sensible person believe the story?

One day over lunch with another rector he struck up conversation about the passage in Colossians that spoke of the letter Paul said he had written to the Laodiceans.

"My sermons next month will include the passage," said Adams. "Most of the commentaries simply say the letter did not survive. I've always wondered what, if anything, we are to make of Paul's reference to Laodicea." He hadn't always wondered anything of the sort, but saying it sounded as if he were continually engaged in ponderous ecclesiastical and theological thinking.

"What if it did survive," he added, "and it simply hasn't turned up yet?"

Surprisingly, his rector friend was a bit more informed than he about the subject, and he spouted off at length about the firm opinion of ancient Jerome that any purported copy of the letter was nothing but a fraud.

"Consider this," he said. "Why do we have copies of the Colossian letter, or the Ephesian letter, or any of the general epistles?"

"I suppose," said Adams, "simply because they were

preserved."

"Well, of *course* they were preserved," said the rector. "We *have* them. But *why* were they preserved? That's the question." He paused for Adams to think it through.

"It would seem their recipients thought them valuable, not just for them but for the church at large," Adams said, proud of his reaching this conclusion.

"Precisely," said the rector. "Paul was a rock star. People hung on his words. Of course, occasionally some people wanted to hang him *for* his words, but I'm talking about the rank and file. They got a letter; they had it copied; and it was copied again and again, in short order."

"If that's true," said Adams, and then corrected himself, "*since* that's true, what does it say that no copies of the Laodicean letter showed up in the first century?"

"Ah! That's the question," said the rector. "It can't be that he didn't write it, because he said he did, and he had no reason to lie about it—if he lied, we're in a bit of trouble with the New Testament, aren't we!"

"Indeed."

"One might propose that whoever received the letter misplaced it, but that doesn't seem at all possible considering the value everyone in the congregation would have placed on it, and the respect they would have had for Paul," said the rector.

"Unless it had been purloined," offered Adams.

"Not likely," said the rector. "In fact, I would find that to be the least likely of any explanation."

Unwittingly, the rector had all but summarily dismissed the story told by the documents themselves in the portfolio. But he then gave his underlying thinking:

"It would've depended on a highly unlikely set of circumstances." He ticked them off on his counted fingers: "A courier who was unreliable; receipt of the letter by someone other than the intended recipient; a sufficient reason for withholding the letter from the church; receipt of the letter by the *exact* person having that reason; and the execution of a plan to hide the letter, if not to destroy it." The rector sat back and looked as satisfied as if he had delivered the winning argument at a forensic debate.

Adams thought, as the rector reeled off this list, that the documents he had read presented just such a series of events as having happened, but he hadn't thought of the fact that each step in that series represented a geometric increase in the improbability that they could all happen and the letter could disappear from history.

Perhaps the Letter to Laodicea was indeed spurious.

Adams changed the subject as casually as he knew how, fearing the rector would wonder if it were just Adam's sermon study that prompted the subject of Laodicea. After all, he might reason that any congregation would be uninspired by a digression about a lost letter of Paul's, and that Adams should know this. In fact, Adams was often clueless that his congregation found his sermons somnolent.

After finishing their light lunch, the two said goodbye and Adams returned to his rectory. He put the matter out of his mind for the rest of the day, and the next. He was not, in fact, going to preach out of Colossians any time soon, and thoughts of the letter became infrequent. The portfolio itself he tucked at the bottom of a cabinet in his office at the church.

Every once in a while, he did think of it, but he couldn't seem to advance his thinking about what to do. He needed someone to help him translate—well, all right, someone to *translate*—the Greek documents and to help decipher the ones written in archaic script. There was a Latin text with no spaces between words and some characters that could easily be one of two or three letters. But he didn't want to involve anyone else, for reasons he had already worked out. Without understanding everything he had, he didn't really know what he would be unveiling to the world if he did. In a quandary, he hoped for some sort of revelation. He would welcome the divine sort, if the Lord so deigned, but simply a light bulb going on in his own head would do.

It was perhaps a dim bulb at best, but light nonetheless, when Adams, who had done absolutely nothing about his valuable or worthless find throughout the rest of 1996 and for more than the next decade, attended a plenary meeting of the Fourteenth Lambast Conference in July of 2008. The decennial, worldwide conference of the Anglican Communion convened at the University of Kent that year, and Adams, who liked to see, and even more to be seen, hobnobbed with some of the nearly seven hundred bishops who were at the meeting as well as rectors who informally audited the conference. In particular, he made the acquaintance of a rector in the American Episcopal Church, who seemed to be of a kindred spirit. He was not very obviously any more erudite than Adams, which put Adams at ease, but neither was he any ruder in education or culture, in spite of the fact that he was an American. Adams liked him.

Adams and the Rev. Ben Thompson (which, in keeping with the anonymity preserved in this account, is not his real name) took lunch together no fewer than four times during the days the meetings were going on, and they became fast friends. Adams hadn't thought for any length of time in the past six months about the treasure or trash he had in an old portfolio in a now junk filled cabinet in his office, and the subject hadn't crossed his mind at the Lambast Conference until something Thompson said to him as they were enjoying treacle tarts for desert. It was just an odd remark about nothing related to Laodicea at all, but about something or other to do with vestments, but Thompson said in jest he was going to "purloin the thing."

Adams's mind immediately went to the claim that someone had purloined the Letter of Paul to the Church at Laodicea.

Immediately, he began wondering if he could afford to take Thompson into his confidence.

Adams turned the conversation to several topics that didn't exactly address the specific topic of Paul's letters but that were designed to scope out Ben Thompson's acumen in the matter of languages, his scholarly skills, and so on. He began to develop some confidence that Ben was a bit better with ancient languages than he, which seemed promising for the prospect of letting him in on the secret.

By the time they needed to get up and go back to the conference site, however, Adams had not worked up to broaching the subject of his strange, secretive, possibly startling, possibly insignificant discovery. Perhaps tomorrow he would make the revelation and take in Thompson as a partner.

Thompson was not to be seen the following day, however, having taken ill, possibly from the tarts, which might have been what upset Adams's stomach that afternoon as well, though not seriously. He was an Englishman, used to the national fare.

In fact, Thompson didn't return to the conference at all. In August, after the meeting had concluded, Thompson wrote a note to Adams apologizing for disappearing suddenly, as he said he had not planned to take in the entire meeting, and had been thankful his return flight plans were made for the day after he fell ill, since his gastro-intestinal upset had tired him greatly. He enjoyed making friends with Adams and hoped they would see each other soon somehow. Perhaps before the next conference, scheduled for 2021, a bit more than the general decade between the worldwide gatherings.

A change of plans

Adams returned correspondence agreeing with the hope that their friendship would continue. No more correspondence ensued until December of that year, after Adams reluctantly went to a physician about an increasingly bothersome bout with what he presumed to be GERD.

In fact, the doctor, who had seen such cases before and known them to turn dark and deadly, immediately scheduled him for some tests, which showed unfortunately that Adams did not have gastroesophageal reflux disease. He had pancreatic cancer. His doctor sat him down and gently told him that he believed Adams had less than three months to live. Stunned but in control for the moment, he asked the doctor if there were treatment. Not at this stage, he was told. Nothing? Not beyond pain relief. Then how will things go?

The physician told him he believed that in Adams's case he would have about another month during which he could control pain with a couple of prescriptions, which would ultimately not be strong enough. At that point he would need sublingual morphine, and ultimately would require medication that would render him incapable of functioning at home, and he would probably have to be admitted to a facility where he could be cared for.

Adams drove home slowly to Lisbeth, his wife of forty-nine years, was unusually quiet during dinner, and then gave in to her patient prodding to tell her what was the matter. They consoled each other throughout the evening and wept silently in the hour it took them to find elusive sleep.

Adams called in to the office and took the following day off. He would have to meet with his solicitor and make certain his will was in perfect order. There were calls to place and decisions to be made. How did people manage this with even less time than he had? How did they hold up while they were finalizing their very lives?

Amidst this flurry of motion, Adams was struck with the realization that he had no plan at all what to do with the portfolio containing the Laodicean letter. Clearly he wouldn't have time to publish it himself. He still hadn't gotten things translated, for one thing.

He could, of course, go to his bishop and simply turn over the material. What would happen to it would happen. But Adams didn't like that idea. He didn't like his bishop. At this point, of course, he wouldn't have to watch the bishop puff up his chest and preen when he announced to the world what he had discovered. Adams would be long gone.

Nor would he be around to see what anyone else would do with the Laodicean letter. But he realized there was only one person he wanted to have the privilege of possessing the secret and deciding whether to bury it or show it to the world: Ben

Thompson.

Adams and his wife Lisbeth had always wanted to holiday in America. It would be a short trip, to be sure, and they wouldn't see much, but it was the only way to accomplish what would be one of his most important acts prior to his death.

The Rev'd William Adams had never told his wife Lisbeth about the Laodicean letter, of course. She hadn't seen the large portfolio. Adams told Lisbeth while they were going through Philadelphia he should like very much to stop in on the Rev. Ben Thompson, a friend he made during the 2008 Lambath Conference and had kept up with since in letters. Lisbeth was not overly curious about it; William had reconnected with a number of people he hadn't seen in years, trying to tie up loose ends, close chapters, make amends, or otherwise say goodbye. She was aware he didn't have many close friends, and if he and this Thompson fellow had established some meaningful bond, she wanted him to enjoy his company in these final hours.

Adams called Ben Thompson, telling him he would be visiting the States shortly and asking to see him one day. Thompson was delighted to hear from Adams, and they agreed upon the day.

Then Adams booked flights to and from the States—arriving in New York and returning from Washington, D.C. He did a little Internet search and selected a hotel in New York, making reservations for the two days he and Lisbeth would be there. From New York, the Adamses would take a train to Philadelphia, where Ben Thompson lived and ministered. The trip was to begin five weeks after Adams received his diagnosis. He prayed he would still be able to function.

Meanwhile, Adams sat down at his little computer and wrote a note to include in the file with all the other notes, documents, and letters. Frightened by what lay ahead of him, he had, in a few short hours, become humbled and he felt very small. His part in the whole Laodicean letter matter was minuscule at best, but he was obligated to say something. He worked over his words for an hour and finally printed out what would have to do:

> I, The Rev'd William Adams of London, England, was caretaker of the Letter of Paul the Apostle to the Church at Laodicea, along with all its attendant documents and letters, from A.D. 1995 until February 2009, at which time I transferred said documents in their entirety to The Rev'd Ben Thompson, of Philadelphia, Pennsylvania, United States.[2]

Adams went on to describe, humbly and in a manner hinting at a sense of shame, how he had acquired the leather portfolio unopened from the Lambath Library. He granted himself a bit

[2] Adams used both his and Thompson's real names.

of defense in saying how the contents of the portfolio made it clear that someone, just *one* someone, was supposed to have taken charge of the materials long ago, and that they should *not* have been opened and made public by a library. He insisted that it was evident that the assistant with whom he had spoken intended to open the locked portfolio, and he inferred that quite obviously, had they been inspected by the Lambath Library staff, they would have been publicized. Adams's actions, he said, while not entirely ethical, had been vindicated (in his opinion).

Adams was aware that he was not painting himself with the brush he would have liked, but his impending death had brought him to a state of honesty with himself about what he had valued and what he had sought in life, and he had become quite confessional in his conversations with family and friends, with Thompson when he shortly read the note, and with the faceless public which would, at some point no doubt, know everything hidden for almost two millennia now.

When he was finished, he printed the letter, read over it, sighed and wept a bit, inserted it in with the other documents, and closed up the thick portfolio for the last time. He would put it in his checked baggage for the flight to America.

15 • Ben Thompson

America was as busy looking a place as London, thought the Adamses as they took a taxi into New York and checked into the hotel they had booked online. It was a whirlwind tour they took of a dozen sights before boarding a train for Philadelphia. The next day Adams made ready to go alone to see his friend, Ben Thompson. When Adams drew the portfolio out of his bag and headed for the hotel room door, Lisbeth asked what it was. He told her it was something he wanted Ben to see. When, in a few hours, he returned without it, Lisbeth either didn't notice or simply didn't ask. She had never been nosy.

Thompson had suggested that Adams meet him at home, but Adams knew he needed privacy for his errand and he suggested he should like to see the church first, so Thompson gave him directions. Adams hailed a cab outside the hotel and read the directions to the driver. The church was well inside the city; there would be cabs driving by it when Adams needed to return to his hotel.

Thompson was waiting for Adams at the top of the church steps when the cab pulled to a stop. The two embraced and then entered the massive oaken front door, disappearing into its darkened interior. After walking through the sanctuary they went to Thompson's offices and closed the door to his study.

Thompson later was to pen only three or four lines about their meeting that morning, without any detail similar to so many caretakers of the Laodicean letter before him. In the first place, he was quietly shocked at Adams's first piece of news, that he was dying, quite rapidly it seemed. Then, when Adams got to the subject of his visit other than friendship, Thompson was simply overwhelmed.

Adams didn't even open the portfolio. He had initially thought he might, but at the moment of revelation he changed his mind. He positioned his hands over it as if it were Pandora's Box, or that he was too deeply reverent to open it. He merely described what was inside.

Then he said when Thompson later studied it, he would understand why Adams didn't want to open it, inspect everything at length, and get involved in the minutia of the various documents on this visit, this last visit. In particular, though he didn't say this to his friend, Adams didn't want Thompson to read his letter in his presence. There would be time enough, when Adams was gone, gone from the church, gone from America, gone from this world, for Thompson to read the confession of Adams and realize the shame with which he passed on the portfolio.

Adams asked Thompson to pledge to him that he would not reveal who had given him the Laodicean materials, until and unless Thompson decided to publish them to the world. Ben said he promised before man and God.

Thompson suggested they go by his home and meet his wife, whom he had told so much about Adams, but Adams was feeling quite tired, was experiencing increasing discomfort at the moment, and had not brought his medication with him. He would need to return to his hotel. This was goodbye. The two shook hands, held their grips motionlessly for a few seconds, needing to wipe their eyes, and then Adams turned, hailed a cab, and was quickly gone.

A scholar at work

Ben Thompson had instantly liked William Adams when they had met in England, despite Adams's trace of hubris and somewhat earthy demeanor. As they had swapped stories and revealed things about their history and experience, Thompson had deliberately played down his love of learning, the value he place on his education, and the devotion he gave to his continuing scholarship. He was content to have found a friend across the Atlantic and he hoped it would be mutually beneficial, even if it were destined to be a long-distance and infrequent friendship.

Thompson had been graduated from the Virginia Theological Seminary in Alexandria, earning the Masters in Divinity and then a doctorate. Though his was not the highest degree he could have sought—he could have gone on to a doctorate in theology elsewhere—he didn't pull the switch on learning once out. He read and studied, practiced his Greek, polished his Latin, and delved into history, becoming a scholar of some local repute in Philadelphia. Though he had not published any books, he had manuscripts of more than a dozen he thought worthy of publication, and he thought he could hold his own with 98% of his fellows in theological pursuits in the Anglican communion and perhaps beyond.

Accordingly, when he began to dig into the documents contained in the ancient portfolio, he didn't feel lost. He didn't feel overwhelmed. He didn't feel out of his element. He felt he had an opportunity laid before him.

He began at the beginning.

The purported Letter to Laodicea—he would regard it as "purported" until and unless he could conclude independently, if possible, that it were genuine—was in tatters, not having been hermetically sealed or cared for as it should have been. It had succumbed to the ancient enemy of parchment: mold. It was not only not readable, in fact, it was in a few hundred bits, most no larger than a dime. The fragments were in some kind of envelope, also quite old, and resembled the pieces of a jigsaw puzzle. Referring to the notes written by Erasmus, which took him a few days to translate reliably, he saw that a second letter, on vellum, had been produced by Erasmus in order to preserve the text itself.

Some of the slight difficulties that would have been presented by the original, which was no longer useful, had been eliminated by Erasmus, who left slight spaces between words and scribed the Greek with a nearly typographical perfection. Thompson set to work on translating the Greek text, using all the tools at his command. Over the next few months, taking what time he could from his busy days, he went to libraries as necessary, made use of Internet resources, and finally completed an English translation he felt was accurate as well as readable. It flowed well without resorting to passing idioms. It was actually more in the style of the King James Version than much more modern versions, owing to Thompson's being steeped in the older English texts. In that respect, it would have fit well with the rest of the New Testament, even though it had never been meant to be the 28th book of the New Testament canon.

He finished with the translation in the late summer of 2009 and began working on the various other Greek notes written by Illyus, Markos Loukios and Basil. They were of a later Greek than the Laodicean letter itself, and they required the same sort of research and patient study. Since they often reverted to the same stylistic difficulties of lettering, some deciphering was required. Occasional words didn't seem to make any sense until he separated them or combined them differently and discovered he had the wrong words to begin with. But finally he succeeded in making what he believed was an accurate translation of all their notes.

Then he took on the Latin documents by Erasmus. The translation Erasmus had done of the Letter to Laodicea itself was less important, Thompson thought, but he tackled it with the same concentration and seriousness he had applied to the Greek. At a few points he thought Erasmus had misconstrued a letter here and there and thus a word here and there, and he trusted his own reading of the Greek. That his reliance on his own reading placed him in contradiction of the likes of Desiderius Erasmus gave him some pause, but he forged on. The differences in the resulting translation, however, were quite slight.

Erasmus's personal notes were more easily translated, having been done in Latin more contemporary to Erasmus himself. Fortunately, Erasmus had not included any notes written in any other language he spoke.

Thompson noted the reasons Erasmus gave for believing the Letter to Laodicea was genuine. Mostly they were an analysis of the original text, its similarity in style to known works of Paul, the probability of its being written in the 1st century, and the sense in which the accompanying documents, particularly those in Koine Greek, attested to the authenticity of the purported letter.

With only a few weeks more study he made sense of the 16th century notes by Colet, which added more weight to his own growing certainty that the letter was genuine. Adams's writings were of little importance in this regard since Adams had done nothing of significance with the entire packet. The best thing he could have done he did: he handed the materials off to someone who could study and evaluate them properly.

There remained in Thompson's mind a thought that while he considered himself competent, a second set of eyes might be valuable at this point, even a team of extra eyes and minds. It was this thinking that gave him pause when he finished his months of work sometime in 2010, and he re-packed the portfolio, interleaving his translations next to the documents translated, and laid it aside for a while. It so happened as well that he was preparing for reassignment, and he became so busy that he had little time to devote to this sideline, as significant as it might be.

The secret is shared

After settling into his new place of service in 2011, the Rev. Ben Thompson made up his mind that he was going to act during the year in the matter of the Laodicean letter. He had done the yeoman's work on all the translating that would have to have been done in order to bring before the world the existence of the ancient document. He certainly wanted to be involved in its publication, as a matter of professional pride. But it went without saying, as a loyal Episcopalian, that his Bishop would have to be involved.

He was aware that if his Bishop was involved, it was likely that the other Bishops would be involved as well. His initial hesitation to go further than privately translating the documents was renewed as he argued with himself about taking the next step. He wouldn't, in a sense couldn't, go forward without involving the bishop, and telling the bishop would open a door that might not be able to be closed again. And what was beyond the door might simply be conflict. But there was nothing else to be done, outside letting the portfolio of precious documents sit in secret indefinitely.

He would tell the bishop.

He hadn't even told his wife. Marianne was a capable counselor and had functioned as such in the parishes he had served. Her strengths lay in interpersonal relationships, however, not ecclesiastical matters. Nor did he want her to be subjected to the temptation to reveal the secret to even just one other. One could never know that the "just one other" person one confided in wouldn't then herself tell "just one other," and soon the secret would be no more.

Ben remembered a conversation between the fictional character Commissioner Frank Reagan on the TV show, *Blue Bloods*. Frank and his daughter Erin are talking in a bar and Erin asks about something mysterious that's going on.

Her father, Frank, says, "Can you keep a secret?"

Erin assures him, "Yes."

Frank comes back, "Good. So can I."[3]

That ended the conversation about the mysterious something. And it stuck in Thompson's mind as a perfect illustration of his philosophy of secrets. If you tell no one else, no one else can tell. So, Thompson wouldn't tell his wife.

But unfortunately he couldn't stick with his own philosophy if he wanted to publish. And after all, if he was going to tell the world shortly, it wouldn't really violate his philosophy of secrets by telling one person to start with. Thompson picked up his phone and scrolled down through his contacts list. He almost never called the bishop, but he did have him listed.

On the basis of Thompson's insistence that it was a matter of some immediate importance, the bishop agreed to see him first thing the next day.

After they engaged in expected pleasantries and Thompson briefly answered the bishop's question as to how things were going so far in his new pastorate, Thompson got down to business.

"Bishop, I have come into possession of something I feel needs to be shared with the whole church—well, the world, really. And I know it would be politic as well as expected that I should share it with you first. In other words, I don't feel I

---

[3] *Blue Bloods*, "Parenthood," S02E12, (Transcript available at: *http:// transcripts.foreverdreaming.org/viewtopic.php?f=196&t=12153*, the Internet).

should go public with it without letting you know. I mean, even if I'm looking for what I would hope would be approval as a formality."

"With an introduction like that," said the bishop, "I'm on full alert."

"No, no, I don't mean to suggest you need to be alarmed," said Thompson. "It's just that—"

"Ben," said the bishop, "Why don't you just tell me what it is?"

"Sure, oh sure," he said. "Well, it's a secret, or at least it's been a secret for a long time. I want to go public."

"Rev. Thompson—"

"Okay, sorry," said Thompson. "Here it is. I received, from one of our brethren in London, a very old Greek manuscript. It's purported to be the lost letter of Paul to Laodicea." Thompson drew a breath and held it.

"What?" said the bishop. "No, I'm sorry. Not 'what'—I'm trying to teach myself not to say that when someone gives me alarming news. Let me begin again. What?!"

Thompson exhaled in a short laugh. "I know. You can't help it."

"No, I could help it, but this surely qualifies for an exception. You have the lost letter. Paul's Epistle to Laodicea."

"That's what I said, yes."

"Where? Here?"

"No, not here. I didn't bring it. But I can, if you want to see it."

"Want to see it?" said the bishop. "Well, of course I want to see it. So I can break it to you gently that you have been had."

"With respect, bishop, I believe I've ruled that out," said Thompson. "I've studied the manuscript and other documents that came with it and—"

"What other documents?"

"Uh, well, notes from people who've had it over the last two thousand years. Librarians, Erasmus, John Colet."

"Erasmus."

"Yes, bishop." Thompson waited to let the news sink in a bit. The bishop looked away and Thompson couldn't tell what he was thinking.

"Erasmus. John Colet. And you," the bishop said.

"I know, I know, I'm nobody," Thompson said.

"Well, I didn't mean you're nobody, but there's no one in this room who would be in the company of men like Colet and Erasmus."

"Agreed," said Thompson. "Which doesn't change the fact that the document was entrusted to me. I can't help my being the low man on the totem pole. I suppose what that means is that I'm honored to be associated with Erasmus."

"Actually, the low man on the totem pole was the most significant, not the least. You're the top man, perhaps," said the bishop. "But that's a secondary thing. The primary thing is that there *is* no such letter. It didn't survive. Somebody is playing a grand trick on you."

"As I said—"

"I know, you don't think so."

"No, I don't. And if you'll mark out some time, I'd like to come back with all the documents and show you why I believe the manuscript is genuine."

"Why didn't you bring them today?"

"I—I didn't really expect this response."

"You didn't expect I would pooh pooh the idea that the Letter to Laodicea somehow survived in secret for 2,000 years and *you* have it?"

Thompson tried to think of another way of answering but couldn't. "Pretty much," he said.

The bishop walked around slowly for a minute, looking at his little library, as if he were going to pull out a book called, "The Letter to Laodicea is a Fake."

"Let's say I'm open to the idea," he said. "Purely hypothetical, mind you. But open, and that I heard you out. If I were to wind up not agreeing with you, I mean *not at all,* what do you think I would say to you about going public?"

"Would you really tell me not to do it?"

"In a heartbeat," said the bishop. "Think of the ramifications for your church, man! Attracting attention to a fraud, convincing the world we're all gullible."

"I don't think it's a fraud."

"But if I did, and if the rest of the bishops did—and I assure you, they would accept my analysis rather than yours—"

"Then the church would disavow me and anything I say. I understand. But why would the church be hurt, then? It would be I who was laughed at."

"The world isn't in the habit of limiting its criticism to the responsible individuals, Ben. It dismisses the whole church for the actions of a few." The bishop had the tone of a slightly perturbed but still patient parent, explaining the way things are to his son.

Thompson let the bishop have his point, and then he presented the alternative.

"What if you were, as you said, open to it, studied the documents with me, and considered my arguments, and afterwards you came to agree with me that the Letter to Laodicea is genuine?"

"Then," said the bishop softly but firmly, "I would even more firmly tell you not to breathe a word of the matter."

"But why?"

"Because the church doesn't *need* another Pauline letter. The Christian *world* doesn't need one. We *have* the New Testament, Ben! Why do you think there aren't three more books in it, or five, or twenty? 'Holy Scripture containeth all things necessary to salvation.' Do you remember your Thirty-Nine Articles, Ben?"

"Of course," said Ben humbly. "But with respect, bishop, I'm not suggesting the church—ours or any other—should print its next version of the New Testament with the Letter to Laodicea in it. I'm just saying if it's genuine, it should be known to scholars everywhere."

"Why? What good will it do? How will it advance the cause of the church? How will it help bring people into the Communion?" The bishop peered into Thompson's eyes, looking for comprehension and ultimately agreement.

"So," said Thompson, "are you telling me that under no circumstance am I to publish my studies of these documents?" He sounded just a slight bit incredulous.

"I am," said the bishop, with calm finality. "I would very much hate to consider the consequences to your ministry if you were to divulge the existence of these documents, let alone any opinion about their authenticity."

Thompson was deflated. He had come to see the bishop thinking that intellectual inquiry would be honored and that the bishop would agree that the world of scholars, if not the people in the pews, should see the letter and decide for themselves what to make of it. It surprised and disappointed him that his bishop held this repressive opinion.

Being a loyal minister, however, committed to the polity of his church, believing that he must submit to the rightful authority over him, he resigned himself, at least for now, to keeping the documents secret. He only hoped the bishop would not attempt to require him to give them to *him.* That would put an end to any hope Thompson had of ever revealing the letter to the world.

"I understand," Thompson said slowly. "Does that mean that you are not even interested in seeing the letter?"

The bishop paused for a few seconds, looking at Thompson, first at one eye, then the other. He realized he had painted himself into something of a corner, saying that no matter whether he praised or panned the letter, he would still tell Thompson not to go public with it. He actually was curious about what the letter said, but if he told Thompson to bring it, he was opening himself to the possibility that he would waver or actually be convinced the letter was genuine, and then he would have to reinforce his present conviction that it should remain secret. If he changed his mind after seeing it, he would look weak. The bishop never enjoyed looking weak.

"I think not," said the bishop. "It wouldn't change my mind."

"I see," said Thompson. "Well, bishop, I'm most grateful for your hearing me out. It helps me to know what your conviction is in the matter."

"Of course, Ben," the bishop said, in a casual and friendly manner, attempting to bring the temperature of the conversation down to normal. He rose, Thompson's cue to get up as well. "Tell your wife—uh, Marianne—hello for me."

"I will, bishop. Thank you."

Thompson left the bishop's chambers and made his way through the darkened halls of the building to the parking lot at the back. As he drove home, one thought occurred to him and planted a seed of hope in him: the bishop was getting old. He was about eighty, and Thompson had heard that the bishop was suffering a decline of some kind, though nobody knew from what. Perhaps Thompson could wait him out. Old bishop dies. New bishop comes into the office. New bishop doesn't know about Thompson's secretive document. Thompson takes another tack and doesn't tell the bishop. It could work.

On reflection, Thompson thought that even if he were reluctant to publish without clearing it by a new bishop, he could always publish anonymously. But where would be the sense of reward in that? No one would know what he had done. It wasn't that he sought glory. Not exactly, anyway. Just credit where credit was due. For all the translation. Not that any other competent scholar couldn't have done that much. Whatever the reason, he wanted his name attached to it.

Before he got home, however, the bishop's argument came back to him. What if the scholarly world didn't agree with him—at all? What if everybody who mattered thought he was a credulous fool? There was no glory in that. Not even credit where credit was due. There was laughing behind his back. And, as the bishop had said, there was harm to the church. To his church. Perhaps to his local parish, or even to his future in the ministry. Especially if the new bishop took it as not only an affront but as a violation of church polity for him to go off and publish a thing without running it by the bishop for approval.

When he turned into his driveway, he was at an impasse with himself. He couldn't see a future anytime soon for publishing. The bishop seemed intractable. There was no guarantee a new bishop would think any different. In fact, it was likely a new one would think like the old one. Perhaps he had just talked himself into imagining public acclaim when it was very unlikely. It certainly appeared that for now, nothing would be done with the manuscript. All the translating was done. There was no more work to be done on the documents. They would sit somewhere in a corner for who knows how long until something happened that would tell Ben Thompson what he was to do with them.

Mid evening, while Marianne was reading, Thompson went upstairs to the bedroom they had agreed would be his study, and he sat down at his desk to write a note. The caretakers of the Letter to Laodicea for 2,000 years had written notes to summarize their actions relating to the letter, leaving these notes in the portfolio they secreted in a library or passed on to another caretaker. Together, the notes told a fairly detailed and fascinating story. At the very least, Thompson would write his own note. If nothing else, this would be his contribution to the chain of custody.

He opened his laptop and started to run his word processor, and then thought better of it. The other caretakers, except for Adams, had written by hand. He would, as well. He pulled out some of his best 32 lb. résumé paper and got out one of his fountain pens, one with a blade nib for doing fine letter calligraphy. Then he wrote several pages of notes, explaining how he came to be the caretaker of the Letter to Laodicea, who gave it to him, and how he had translated the documents. He gave a brief, diplomatic summation of his bishop's directions, and then he indicated that as of this writing, the letter would remain secret, until by the hand of God it became clear he must do otherwise.

Satisfied with his work, he slipped his note in with the other documents. Before packing them all up the last time, he enclosed every document in its own protective plastic sheet. He folded the portfolio closed, engaged the locks that didn't lock, and found a place in the bottom of the file drawer in his desk, beneath manilla envelopes stuffed with items of little consequence, little boxes filled with pens and pencils never used, and other things collected over the years and likely not to be disturbed anytime soon. When the drawer was closed, Thompson left the room, turned out the light, went to bed, and lived until 2018 before digging back down into the drawer to retrieve the ancient letter.

Ecumenical friendship

In 2017 Ben Thompson wrote a book. It was a commentary on Hosea intended for the person in the pew. While Thompson was fully capable of writing a scholarly work, over the years he had been more and more convinced that if the laity as well as the clergy knew the scriptures better, the church would be stronger and probably greater in numbers. He was having difficulty finding a publisher for the work, however, having written half a dozen query letters and having gotten half a dozen nicely worded rejections. Convinced he needed help in putting his best foot forward to convince editors to read his manuscript, in early 2018 he signed up for a writer's conference in Richmond, Virginia, in the early summer of that year. The website for the conference promised writers lots of networking opportunities with other writers, a shot at pitching their books to agents attending, helpful presentations, *and much more!* They always said that.

When the conference week in June arrived, Ben packed his bags for the drive down to Richmond. He would be staying in the hotel where the event was taking place in its conference rooms. Marianne stayed at home, planning actually to visit an old college friend in Kennett Square. During the evenings there would be no conference events, so he would be on his own. There wasn't much on television that Ben Thompson liked these days, so there wouldn't be much to do. The drinkers at the conference would populate the bars, in the hotel and out, but Thompson was not a drinker. He could take a book or two to read, but he didn't have anything new just now. Well, he could pick up a paperback at the hotel shop.

A curious and surprising thought occurred to him. Suppose he took the Laodicean materials. He hadn't looked at them in quite some time, and he might want to read over his translations and see if they sounded as good as he thought when he first did them in 2011. Or he might revise or add to his own notes, perhaps to explain why he continued to keep them secret. It was an odd thought and an odd idea to take study-type materials to occupy a relaxation time. Nevertheless, he went up to his study, dug to the bottom of the file drawer in his desk, retrieved the portfolio, and put it in his suitcase. The bulk forced him to take another small bag in order to pack enough for the conference days.

Then he put his bags in the car, kissed his wife, and drove the four and a half hours down I-95 to Richmond, arriving in time to check in by 4:00 p.m. He registered before 6:00. The meetings began in the morning.

At the first day of the conference, there were seminars on a variety of topics from writing for beginners, to finding an agent, to navigating contract negotiations with publishers. At 10 a.m.,Thompson went to the well attended "Getting Past the Rejection Letter" seminar, finding one of the few seats available near the back. He sat down by a man about his age—70, he was afraid—and at the first break he introduced himself.

Thompson's new friend was Wade Vaughn, a Baptist, retired from active ministry and trying to get published by someone other than a denominational entity. He had seen some little things get published by his convention's press, for paltry sums, no royalties, and he really believed his writing was worth a wider readership and a better return.

Thompson shared the same conviction, and he briefly described his latest writing, the commentary on Hosea. As the break came to an end, they agreed to eat lunch together when the morning seminars ended at noon. They attended different seminars at 11 a.m., and then met up in the hotel lobby at 12.

The large hotel had two fine restaurants in it, so they picked the one that was likely to have light lunch options. While waiting for their orders, they were having a casual debate about the advantages and disadvantages of their respective church polities. Thompson made a remark about something he "would have to run by his bishop."

"I couldn't deal with that," said Vaughn. "We Baptists love our individual autonomy just about as much as the Bible," he said. "Not really, but it's way up there on the list. You want a fight with a Baptist preacher, try telling him that he has to kowtow to the local Baptist Association or State Convention. He'll put you in your place real quick."

Thompson smiled and sipped his tea—his unsweet, the southerner Wade Vaughn's, extra sweet—but while he sipped, he was processing the thought that had suddenly occurred to him.

Ben Thompson wasn't going to do anything with the Letter to Laodicea. He now knew that. He had waited around seven years thinking his bishop would go on to be with the Lord and another bishop, perhaps more open to the subject of the letter, would take his place. But his bishop had been healed, apparently, of whatever ailed him in 2011, seemed to have a new lease on life, and plowed on with unusual strength for a man of eighty-five or six or seven.

Ben, on the other hand, was running into a plethora of indications that even at seventy-one, he was aging fast. He didn't know that he had some disease hiding out in one of his organs or waiting to ambush him one morning and send him to the hospital not to return, but he didn't know that he didn't have such, either.

Over the years since he had taken possession of the old manuscripts, and after the initial, furious flurry of work he had done on them, Ben had become almost indifferent to what happened to them. Sometimes he thought his bishop was right: that if the letter was a fake, he shouldn't publish it, and if it was genuine, he still shouldn't publish it. What was the use, after all? Other times, he reverted to that first instinct, probably out of pride, to get the notoriety, the fame, for announcing to the world the existence of the missing letter of Paul. More and more, he had difficulty justifying that desire for its own sake. Less and less sure of whether he should do anything at all with the letter, he had left it buried in his file drawer for all this time and his once energetic intention to make a name for himself had dwindled to nearly nothing.

But here in his new friend, Wade Vaughn, his Baptist friend, his rebel with a cause, maybe here was someone who would do what Thompson had come to believe he would not, should not, could not do. Perhaps God had put them together at this conference. This wasn't a Christians-only conference; it was a writer's conference. There were probably women attending who were witches trying to get books of potions published, or men trying to get published to convince the world there was no God. How come Thompson had sat down by a Baptist minister? Maybe God had put them in the same seminar, in seats beside each other, and inspired his friend to praise the independence and autonomy of Baptists, just so Thompson would realize this was the hour to pass the baton.

Their orders came, and they dug in for a spell, chitchatting about the conference presenters. Thompson was teetering on the fulcrum of decision, and finally decided this was the time to pass off the letter to someone else. The Persians would call it kismet. It probably fit into the vague definition of the Hindu's karma. For Ben Thompson, he was convinced it was divine providence. This was what he was supposed to do, at this point in his little part of history. God had provided a runner to take the baton.

Perhaps he would ask for credit due when the time came, perhaps not. Maybe he would never see what transpired, if anything. He put down his fork.

"I have something to give you, Wade," Thompson said.

"What are you talking about?" said Vaughn.

"When we finish here in a minute, come up to my room."

In Thompson's room within fifteen minutes, he retrieved the portfolio from his bag and placed it on a table provided in the sitting area. The two stood over it and Thompson undid the clasps and opened the old leather folder.

"That's a very interesting portfolio," said Vaughn. "Looks custom made. Heavier than any I've seen before."

"It's quite old," said Thompson. "The locks don't work anymore, but whatever."

Thompson pulled out the sheaf of papers in plastic sleeves. His own note was on top, and he moved it to the side and turned it over casually. Time enough later for Wade to read it.

He turned to the last page, not counting the envelope containing a hundred pieces or more of crumbling parchment. The pages were Erasmus's copy of the letter.

"Wow," said Wade quietly. "That's old. That looks like it might be an old manuscript portion of the New Testament." He looked at Thompson with wide eyes. "*Is it?*"

"Not exactly," said Thompson. "Are you ready for this? This is the Letter of the Apostle Paul to the Church at Laodicea. The real thing. At least, I'm convinced it is." Thompson held the up the protector, which contained the four pages of Erasmus's copy of the original, and Wade Vaughn looked at it and then looked up with some confusion.

"Wait," he said, "what letter?"

"The letter Paul said he wrote."

"That letter was lost," he said.

"Yes, it was," he said. "Let's just say it's like the scripture says about the Prodigal Son: 'Once it was lost, but now it is found.'"

"It can't be. Just can't."

"I assure you it can," said Thompson. "Give me a chance to explain how."

"Uh, okay."

"It's a long story, and it's all in here, all these pages. I'll give you an overview."

They sat down on short sofas facing each other on either side of the table, and Thompson began at the beginning, going over the notes written by Illyus of Antioch about a strange visit from Akakios, a man in the Laodicean church. Thompson covered the broad sweep of the story, finally coming to his own receipt of the portfolio a few years ago, and his quandary after meeting with his bishop. When he finished, he just became quiet and waited for some kind of response.

"Again, wow," said Vaughn. "And you've come to the conclusion that it's genuine?"

"I have."

"But you weren't allowed to—at least you didn't—consult with any other scholars?" Vaughn said, not at all in an accusatory way.

"No. No one before me had really done so, not without handing the materials off completely, like Markos Loukios did. I didn't think it was wise, at least until I was ready to go public.

And I've realized, to my distress, that I'm not the one to go public with the letter."

"But you want me to have a copy of something? Surely not of the letter itself?"

"No, you don't understand. I want you to have the entire portfolio. The letter, all the translations, all the notes, everything."

"Oh, Ben, no! I couldn't. I can't. I mean—"

"I know, I know. I felt the same way when Rev. Adams gave it to me. I didn't say much, actually. I was too dumbfounded. But I finally realized it wasn't about me. It was about him. It was something he *had* to do. I couldn't say No without denying him the opportunity—really, for him, the obligation—to do God's will."

"You're saying you think it's God's will for you to pass this on to me?"

"Yes," said Thompson. He described the events that had led up to this decision and said, "I think this was God speaking."

Being a Baptist, tending to place a great deal of importance on the dynamic experience of faith and the moving of the Holy Spirit, hoping every day to hear God speak in some way, Wade Vaughn did not easily dismiss another Christian's solemn statement that he was acting at the direction of God.

He did have a question, however.

"What am I to do with it?" he said.

"That's not up to me," said Thompson. "That will be up to

you. You are freer than I am in your church. But you're just as free *not* to do something as you are to do it."

"What if I buried it?"

"Free to do that."

"What if I don't agree with you that it's authentic?"

"You're free to reach your own conclusion, Wade."

"What if I just published the whole story and said, 'Make your own minds up, folks; I'm just putting it out there for everybody to see.'"

"If that's what you think needs to be done," said Thompson.

Wade sat back and put his hands out over the back of the sofa to each side, stared at Thompson, and shook his head slowly and slightly in an expression of disbelief. Thompson slowly stacked the documents in their proper order and inserted them in the enclosure on the right side of the portfolio. The silk lining was beginning to rot a bit here and there. He closed the portfolio, folded over the straps, and then slowly slid it to the center of the table.

"The only request I make of you," said Thompson, "is that until and unless you make all the documents public, that you not reveal who gave them to you. If you publish them, I will take my chances then on being mentioned as part of the custodial chain."

"I could leave you out, even then," said Vaughn. "Just make up a name and leave it vague."

"That's up to you," said Thompson. "I used to think, 'credit where credit is due,' but now I think I have been wrong. It doesn't matter to me anymore."

Vaughn leaned forward and put his hand on the portfolio, drawing it slowly to his side. It crossed his mind one more time to say he couldn't do it, but he was convinced that this new friend of his had gone through some deep soul-searching about the matter, and he wouldn't insult him. If, after studying everything exhaustively, he thought it was an ancient, well-done, but thorough hoax, all he had to do was to bury it, figuratively or quite literally. But there was always the possibility that it wasn't a hoax at all.

Vaughn picked up the portfolio and stood. "I have to go to my room on six before going to an afternoon presentation. I'm going to the one on finding an agent. You?"

"Possibly," said Thompson. "I may be late to whatever I attend."

"Maybe we'll take the same seminar tomorrow," said Vaughn. "Let's be sure to talk again before we leave."

"Of course," said Thompson, and the two walked to his room door. Vaughn went out and strode down to the elevator. Thompson closed the door, went to his bed, laid out on his back on top of the spread, and sobbed quietly, both in grief for his not being the one to reveal the secret to the world, and relief for his being free of the burden to make that decision and risk the public response.

16 • STEVEN R. FRANCES

AND SO IT COMES FULL CIRCLE. Wade didn't wax confessional in the notes he included with the rest of the documents and the letter. Only to me did he profess to be incompetent to evaluate provenance, organize the materials, and construct some cogent presentation to the world of what he had. His contribution was a lengthy summary that included what, contrary to his self-effacing remarks, were quite insightful comments on the history of the Laodicean Letter. But he had finally found himself so nervous about going public that he seized on a coincidental article by an almost long-lost friend to conclude that he should hand off the Laodicean mystery to me.

Wade essentially called the coincidence a "God thing." Maybe, maybe not. It is what it is. I have it, and now I'm about give it, and the story of its provenance to the Christian world, a world that isn't particularly concerned about the ancient mystery and isn't waiting breathlessly for a revelation that will solve it. Its that *provenance* that I said the reader would have to evaluate.

I return to a hesitant figure crouched over his shredder, a nightmare-wakened nobody, desperate to know if he really destroyed invaluable documents, and a relieved old man, nervously determined to uncover a two-millennia secret, for good or ill to him.

He is me. Or I. It doesn't matter. As I said to begin with, I decided that I didn't have the moral right either to conceal or to destroy the Laodicean letter. In a real sense, it doesn't belong to me. I have merely been its caretaker for a little while. The Epistle of the Apostle Paul to the Church at Laodicea belongs to the world. To the Christian world, and to the world beyond.

And as I said to begin with, it isn't up to me to decide anything for you. You the reader are the trier of fact. You are the ultimate jury. It's up to you to conclude that the letter is a fraud, or is genuine. I've decided my role is simply to put forth the history as others have told it, therewith to make the case for it, and to print the letter. And so, I do.

17 • THE LETTER

THE LETTER OF THE APOSTLE PAUL to the Church at Laodicea was written in Koine Greek. The original letter was stored with insufficient care by Akakios, who purloined it, Illyus, who did not know it was a letter, and also by Markos Loukios, who handled it a thousand years later. By the 16th Century it was in several pieces, but by the 20th century it was virtually shredded. If it had not been for the careful work of Erasmus, who made an exact copy of it, it would be useless.

The Greek was first translated into English in 2009 by the Rev. Ben Thompson, who deliberately styled the text to be similar to the King James Version of the Bible. I have not revised what he did to make it sound more modern.

- *If* the Letter to the Laodiceans had been delivered to the Church at Laodicea per plan; and
- *If* it been copied and circulated as other Pauline letters were; and

- *If* it had been included by Athanasius of Alexandria in his proposed list of the New Testament canon in A.D. 367; and
- *If* it had been accepted by the church at the Council of Rome in A.D. 382 and the Council of Florence in 1439; then
- It would have appeared in the New Testament, first the Latin Vulgate, then the English versions—Wycliffe, Tyndale, the Great Bible, the King James Version—and down to the present day. Perhaps it would have appeared in the order of books right after Colossians. Every Sunday School child who learns the books of the New Testament, how "Galatians, Ephesians, Philippians, Colossians" flows so trippingly on the tongue, would have only to add "Laodiceans" to the mix.

None of these things happened. We must assume, as Wade Vaughn said, that the Laodicean letter was not meant by the Holy Spirit to be in the canon. Surely, if God had wanted this writing of Paul included in the general epistles of Paul that Christians should read, study and obey throughout this present age, he would have frustrated the attempts of Akakios to conceal the writing.

For instance, if only Illyus of Antioch, sufficiently concerned about the motives of his acquaintance, Akakios, in having him hide a leather pouch, and almost certain that the pouch contained information either embarrassing or incriminating to Akakios, had opened it and discovered what it was, history would have been different.

If Erasmus, who went so far as to translate the original Greek manuscript into Latin, had published either the Latin or the Greek or both, history would have been different.

If John Colet had not allowed his misgivings about the possible effect of publishing the manuscript keep him from doing so as the Protestant Reformation was heating up, history would have been different.

By the time a nameless librarian's assistant noticed a volume in the Lambath Library labeled, "John Colet: Correspondence," and mentioned it to his rector, it was too late for history to feel much of a tremor because of the uncovering of an ancient letter.

And I do not expect the Richter Scale of the theological world, much less the world at large, to register any signal at all in my publishing the letter. After all, as I said before, and as several caretakers of the letter along the way have said, the letter adds nothing to the doctrines of the Bible, Old Testament or New. It doesn't contradict anything Paul or any other Bible author said. It reflects the same style and the same thoughts from the same time period as the general epistles. And the New Testament has done quite well, thank you, as the word of God, along with the Old Testament, for 2,000 years, and will suffice until Jesus comes again.

Nevertheless, for whatever interest it holds for anyone

anywhere, I reproduce the English translation here. And as classic affidavits still sometimes say in closing: "Further affiant sayeth not." There's nothing left for me to say. The verdict is in your hands.

Steven R Francis

THE EPISTLE OF PAUL TO THE

LAODICEANS

Paul, an apostle of the Lord
Jesus Christ by the will of
God, to the saints which are at
Laodicea,
2 Grace be to you from God
our Father and the Lord Jesus
Christ,
3 Who hath chosen you in himself for obedience in faith, that
you might be his witnesses to the
gospel we preach:
4 That Christ hath become our
Saviour by his blood, and hath
been proclaimed our Lord
through his resurrection from
the dead.
5 Which ye believed, having
confessed that he is Lord, and
having been baptized into him.
6 How is it now that ye have
been lured into sin by one who
would deceive you?
7 For I hear that Akakios hath
crept into your number
unawares, teaching you after the
manner of Nicolas,
8 Who leadeth men to deny not
the flesh, but rather to join with
the pagans, reveling in their
wickedness .
9 And this he does that he
might gain friendship of the
world, and that he might also
gain a good degree of them that
rule, and that he might be rich.
10 But fornication and lascivi-
ousness are idolatry; and God
hath called us to holiness, and to
forsake uncleanness and covetousness.
11 How then are you so easily
deceived, in going after that
which is carnal?
12 For Christ died for our sins,
and he rose that he might be
Lord. If then ye confess the
Lord Jesus Christ, how dost thou
live any longer in the lusts of thy
flesh?
13 Be not deceived therefore by
them which teach things they
ought not, but rather continue
in the things ye have been taught
by them who first preached the
gospel of Christ to you.
14 And as ye heard that Christ is
Lord, so walk worthy of God
and of the gospel of Christ, for
this will bring a good report.

CHAPTER 2

1 For the Son is the image of

the invisible God, for whom all
things were created, and whom
all creation shall confess, that he
is Lord.
2 For of his great love for us
Christ emptied himself and became like us, and died for us that
we might live unto God,
3 And that we might be delivered from this present, evil world
through the power of the Holy
Ghost.
4 And for this reason hath God
called you to walk in love toward
all men, and especially toward
them that are of the faith.
5 For we must love one another
as Christ hath loved us.
6 And God hath called us to a
ministry of love in the gospel of
Jesus Christ, that they who are
the servants of idols might know
the truth.
7 This gospel hath gone out
into the world and hath borne
fruit, as men hear the word of
truth.
8 And so have ye in the past
made known the glorious gospel,
such that many repented and
believed and were saved.
9 But they that love this world
are faithless, and love not the
Lord Jesus Christ.
10 They are ashamed of the testimony of our Lord, fearing
them that worship idols or them
that are of the circumcision.
11 Therefore the sound of the
gospel is not heard where a spirit
of fear hath come over them that
believe.
12 Strengthen yourselves, therefore, girded with the truth, and
build up each other in love, en-
couraging one another in your
worship, and in your fellowship
with one another.
13 Fill yourselves with knowledge through the word of God,
that you might stand against the
darkness of this world.
14 Rejoice in the Lord and in the
hope of the glory of God that
comes through Jesus Christ.
15 Pray for one another, that ye
may be strengthened with his
might, against every deception
and stronghold of the adversary.
16 Worship God in the Spirit,
that ye may also walk in the Spirit, to the glory of God.
17 And pray for us, for we labour
in bonds; for I am a prisoner of
Christ.
18 Pray that though I am in

bonds the word of the Lord
might have free course.
19 And if we be not delivered to
visit you, pray that we may hold
fast unto the end, in nothing
ashamed.
20 For whether we live or die, we
are confident that all things shall
fall out unto the furtherance of
the gospel and the praise of Jesus
Christ.

CHAPTER 3

1 I would that ye knew, brethren, how I long after you, that
ye may understand the mystery
of God the Father and of Christ:
that in Christ all the fulness of
God dwelleth;
2 And that ye might be filled
with the Spirit continually, that
ye might shine as lights in the
world, as God hath shined upon
you.
3 And to this end God hath
given you ministers of the word,
which have laboured among you
faithfully.
4 I exhort you to honour them,
that their ministry might be
profitable among you.
5 Epaphras saluteth you, who
hath laboured there, and in
Colossae.
6 Tychicus saluteth you, a
brother beloved in the Lord and
a fellowworker with me.
7 To Nymphas, who laboureth
in the ministry for your profit, I
write this in my own hand.
8 The love of God our Father,
the grace of our Lord Jesus
Christ, and the communion of
the Holy Ghost be with you all.
Amen.

www.ingramcontent.com/pod-product-compliance
Lightning Source LLC
Chambersburg PA
CBHW030815310726
48980CB00006B/508/J
9780999592960